"Don't apologize." Asim breathed deep, filling the void in his lungs. "I don't like it when you're...meek." The words surprised him as much as her. He felt the shock of that admission reverberate through him, even as he saw it ripple across Jacqui's face.

He didn't approve of the way she argued with him, refusing to be silenced after he'd made a decision. It happened daily when she tried to wheedle access to records or palace staff or ancient pavilions that had been locked up as unsafe generations ago. Yet seeing her hesitant and downcast was like watching a bright light dim.

For long seconds their eyes locked. Long enough for him to notice that in the syrupy late-afternoon light her eyes flashed with shards of gold.

Slowly her mouth eased into a crooked smile.

"In that case, Asim..." Jacqui paused over his name as if savoring it. "I promise not to be meek with you again."

She scooped up her towel and wrapped it around herself, hurrying toward her room. But her chin was up and her shoulders back and, despite his body's howl of protest at her departure, Asim found himself smiling.

Desert Vows

Two powerful desert princes...and the only women who can tame them.

Sultan Asim of Jazeer and Sheikh Tariq of Al-Sarath are both bound by honor, duty and tradition. They've always known they must marry, but it would be for the good of their kingdoms—*not* for love. Yet now two very different women threaten the vows Asim and Tariq have always sworn to uphold.

As desire burns hotter than the desert sand, can these powerful sheikhs withstand the heat of temptation?

Find out in:

The Sultan's Harem Bride

February 2015

The Sheikh's Princess Bride

April 2015

Annie West

The Sultan's Harem Bride

Recycling programs
for this product may
not exist in your area.

ISBN-13: 978-0-373-13314-7

The Sultan's Harem Bride

First North American Publication 2015

Printed in U.S.A.

Growing up near the beach, **Annie West** spent lots of time observing tall, burnished lifeguards—early research! Now she spends her days fantasizing about gorgeous men and their love lives. Annie has been a reader all her life. She also loves travel, long walks, good company and great food. You can contact her at annie@annie-west.com or PO Box 1041, Warners Bay, NSW 2282 Australia.

Other titles by Annie West available in ebook:

DAMASO CLAIMS HIS HEIR
AN ENTICING DEBT TO PAY
(At His Service)
IMPRISONED BY A VOW
CAPTIVE IN THE SPOTLIGHT
DEFYING HER DESERT DUTY
UNDONE BY HIS TOUCH
(Dark-Hearted Tycoons)
GIRL IN THE BEDOUIN TENT
(Sinful Desert Nights)
PRINCE OF SCANDAL
PASSION, PURITY AND THE PRINCE
(The Weight of the Crown)
SCANDAL: HIS MAJESTY'S LOVE-CHILD
(Dark-Hearted Desert Men)
FORGOTTEN MISTRESS, SECRET LOVE-CHILD
(Regally Wed)
THE SAVAKIS MISTRESS
(Tall, Dark and Dangerously Sexy)
BLACKMAILED BRIDE, INNOCENT WIFE
(Innocent Wives)
THE DESERT KING'S PREGNANT BRIDE
(Unexpected Babies)

To my dear friend Karen
with love and thanks, not just for now, but always.

CHAPTER ONE

'GIVE IT UP, JACK. This is a wild goose chase.' Imran's voice came over the hubbub of vehicles, people and livestock thronging the pre-election cavalcade.

'No!' Jacqui shook her head. 'You'll see. It will be worth it.'

It *had* to be worth it. They had a chance to interview one of the world's most hard to meet opposition leaders, an inspirational reformer the authorities would do anything to silence. It was an opportunity not to be missed.

Yet uneasiness stirred. This jammed street was strangely familiar, as if she'd been here before. The pungent aromas of dust, sweat, spices and dung teased her nostrils. A disturbing sense of *déjà vu* made her pause.

Jacqui swung round, looking for Imran's familiar face.

Anxiety speared her. Her nape prickled. 'Imran?'

'Right here, Jack.' She spun round and there he was, large as life, his camera over one shoulder, his laughing eyes narrowed against the sun.

Relief thudded in her chest. For a moment Jacqui had feared... Feared what? Her train of thought dissolved.

'This is a long shot, despite the tip-off,' she said. 'If you'd rather go to the hotel, I'll try to locate him then call you.'

Imran's expression didn't change.

Had she spoken aloud or just thought about it? Confused, she lifted a hand to her hot forehead. Everything felt unreal, strangely distant. Even the faces of the people around them seemed blurred.

All except Imran.

Jacqui blinked and tried to focus. The job. The lead. This would be their best story yet. Their news editor wouldn't believe it if they came in with this exclusive.

It was an opportunity to reveal the truth about this oppressive regime. Then world powers could no longer plead ignorance and turn a blind eye to the violence.

'Come on, Jack. Don't dawdle.' Imran strode ahead, forging easily through the packed street.

Jacqui tried to follow but her feet seemed stuck to the ground, her limbs weighted. With a supreme effort, she struggled forward a pace. Just one. Around her the crowd slowed too, like a film moving frame by frame.

All except Imran, striding through the barely moving people. Each step took him further away.

Jacqui opened her mouth to call his name, urge him to stop. The *déjà vu* was back, stronger this time. Her flesh crawled in horrified premonition. Her throat constricted, silencing her strained vocal cords.

Helplessly she watched him meld into the crowd.

Then it came. The nameless thing she'd been expecting without knowing. A soundless judder of vibration on the air. A quake that made the ground beneath her feet shudder and heave.

Then the cataclysmic roar. A deafening well of sound, spiralling round her. So loud her ears rang and kept on ringing.

Finally her stasis broke. She ran, lungs pumping, breath tearing in her throat. Still she couldn't call out.

She slammed to a stop. Imran's camera lay on the ground, its shattered lens glinting in dusty sunlight. He held it fast, fingers clamped round it.

Jacqui knelt, her brain trying to make sense of the picture before her. The ungainly jumble of limbs, the shapes impossible to comprehend. An unholy cocktail of dust and bright-red liquid spread all round her, soaking the ground, filling her nostrils.

She put out a hand to touch what had once been the man she knew better than anyone. A man fit, whole...

Finally she found her voice. It rose, filling the air, an anguished, wordless scream.

Asim stalked the empty corridor and out into a moonlit courtyard. Annoyance lengthened his stride and made the blood steam in his veins.

What had possessed his ambassador to suggest that woman as a possible bride? Or hint to the old Emir that he should bring his niece? This should have been a simple state visit to finalise an energy venture between their countries. Instead the Emir's visit to Jazeer was a potential diplomatic disaster.

Asim strode past the scented garden and into another passage. The sprawling old palace provided plenty of space to be alone with his impatience.

Not as good as the freedom of a four-wheel drive on the desert dunes but that luxury was denied him. Asim had to remain here to play host to the Emir and his unwanted niece in the morning. He'd need to soothe the Emir's pride but make it clear his choice of bride lay elsewhere.

He grimaced. If beauty were all he required, she might have been a contender. She was one of the most flagrantly gorgeous women he'd met.

That was saying something. In his youth, Asim had acquired a well-deserved reputation as a connoisseur of beautiful women. Blonde, brunette, redhead, slim, curvaceous, tall or petite. He'd enjoyed them all.

Did they believe he'd be so seduced by her charms he'd ignore her character? She'd been demure tonight. But Asim knew that in the exclusive holiday hideaways of the mega-wealthy she had an unrivalled reputation for pleasure, for multiple lovers and chemical stimulants.

Only a fool could think he'd turn a blind eye to that!

The woman Asim married would become wife to the Sultan of Jazeer. She would be intelligent, beautiful and capable; a devoted mother. She would be a woman of dignity and self-control, of impeccable standards. Not the subject of salacious gossip.

His wife would be everything his mother hadn't been.

Oh, she had been beautiful. And loving, in her own way.

An icy finger tracked down Asim's spine.

Fate preserve him from *love*!

That curse had destroyed his parents and now his sister. He had no intention of suffering a similar destiny.

He drew a slow breath. He'd hoped to keep his decision to acquire a wife quiet. Now speculation would be rife and he'd be bombarded with hopeful candidates.

A sharp cry brought Asim up short. He lifted his head, searching for its source.

It came again, an unearthly shriek on the still night air, raising the hairs on the back of his neck. It wasn't a peacock, or a wild dog beyond the city outskirts.

Asim strode down an arched passageway to an even older building, long disused. The cry sounded again as he emerged into a space wilder and less formal than the other gardens.

He knew this place. As a boy he'd listened to the old stories of tragedy and avidly watched for proof that the garden was, indeed, haunted.

Now, at thirty-five, Asim didn't consider the possibility of meeting a ghost. He was more concerned with the flesh and blood source of that scream.

It came again. High, anguished, wordless. Its tenor of distress catapulted him forward. As he neared the pavilion on the far side of the garden a glow caught his eye and adrenalin pumped hard in his blood.

Asim sprinted towards the light. Fire in the centuries-old building would be disastrous.

Yet there was no scent of smoke, no crackle of burning. Perhaps the flames hadn't taken hold.

He slammed through a wide entrance, past dark, empty rooms to a doorway spilling light.

He jerked to a stop, heart pounding. The peace of the scene before him, after the turmoil he'd expected, flummoxed him for a moment and he strove to take it in.

An old-fashioned hanging lamp sent shafts of multi-hued light across the wall murals and inlaid floor. The place was bare of furniture but for a small table, a carved chest and a bed.

It was the bed that caught his attention. He stared, disbelieving, at the woman who lay naked upon it.

Asim sucked in an astonished breath, his fingers curling around the door jamb.

Lamplight painted her bare flesh in delicate rainbow hues. Gold across her long, slim legs, lithe and restless. Rose at her hips, over her smooth, pale belly and the V of reddish-brown pubic hair. Lavender across the perfect swell of firm, high breasts that shook and trembled with her agitated breathing. Pale azure over her neat jaw, slender throat and contorting mouth.

Surprise, curiosity and a surge of raw masculine hunger warred within him at the enticing picture she presented.

With her arms raised high above her head on a satin cushion, she looked like some delectable feast laid out for his enjoyment—an invitation to touch and taste.

Sexual arousal slammed into him, congealing thought.

Asim swallowed as his groin tightened and his blood rushed faster. His gaze drifted from the swell of her dainty breasts to her shifting thighs.

Heaving an unsteady breath, he grappled back to sanity and strode forward.

Spikes of damp, tawny hair splayed over the pillow as she tossed her head. Her throat worked and a soft mew emerged from her lips. It had to be a sound of distress, yet some primitive part of him wondered if that was how she'd sound in the throes of passion.

Heat rose from her. Asim felt it as he stood beside her.

Deliberately he clasped his hands behind his back, conquering the base instinct that made him want to reach out.

He should comfort her. But the compulsion to touch sprang as much from the need to know if her creamy skin was as soft as it looked.

Asim scrubbed an unsteady palm over his face, forcing down impulses that could only be dishonourable.

Who was this woman?

What was she doing in the most ancient part of his palace, alone and naked?

Despite the gravity of his royal position some women had gone to inordinate lengths to offer themselves to him.

Was she one of them? Was this her idea of a tantalising new twist on the age-old mating ritual?

His body's reaction showed she'd succeeded in piquing his interest.

In his wilder youth he might have been tempted by such a tactic. But it was a wife he sought now, not a one-night stand.

Inevitably his gaze was drawn back to her body. She was slim almost to the point of thinness. A model? She was tall enough. Yet she was completely unadorned—not even a ring or gold chain.

He didn't know a woman who didn't wear some jewellery, even if just stud earrings.

She was so…bare.

Yet there was no mistaking the powerful tide of desire sweeping him. The dragging weight in his lower body. His heartbeat's thrum of anticipation. His rapid breathing.

Asim stretched out his arm. He opened his hand a metre above her and imagined he felt the scrape of one pebbled nipple tease his palm. A jolt of electricity rushed from his fingers, up his arm and straight to his groin. He fisted his hand against the urge to reach down and cup her *there*.

Abruptly she moved, scrabbling at the sides of the bed. Her head twisted. She drew an enormous breath that hollowed her belly and thrust her tip-tilted breasts towards him as a muffled sob broke from her lips.

Asim reared back, shame and disbelief scalding him. He'd been acting the voyeur!

'It's time to wake up,' he said, his voice assuming a familiar tone of firm command.

Asim's mouth twisted. If only he'd had such command over his own cruder impulses.

He opened his mouth to repeat the order when she gasped, writhed and screamed at the top of her lungs.

'It's time to wake...time to wake.' The words circled Jacqui's brain like a half-forgotten mantra. The ground shook again, heaving her up and down, a boneless rag doll. She didn't run. Where could she escape to? Why should she? She'd led Imran into danger and now he was dead. How could she even think about surviving herself?

Heat suffused her like an embrace, at odds with the chill in her bones. Still she clung to Imran's hand, wishing she could rewind time. For nothing, she knew, could bring him back from this.

But that voice was insistent, ordering her to pay attention, ordering her to...wake.

The deafening sound stopped abruptly. It took Jacqui a while to realise it was the sound of her own screams. Her throat was raw and her chest heaved. Fear clawed, though the worst panic began to subside.

She'd done this before. She knew what it meant. She'd had one of her dreams. Even as she told herself *this* was reality, this quiet, peaceful place, her brain buzzed anxiously.

'That's better.' It was the voice again. Low, soothing, so deep it shivered right to the core of her. 'You're awake now, aren't you?'

For a moment longer she could swear she grasped Imran's still-warm hand. Then the sensation faded.

He was gone. Grief scooped a hollow in her belly.

Tears flooded her eyes and spilled down her cheeks. Stupid, helpless tears that came too easily now. She rubbed her hand across her face, smearing wetness, trying to scrub it away. A choking ball of emotion lodged in her throat and she swallowed clumsily, heedless of the pain.

Something shifted. The heat on her shoulders abated. Belatedly she realised it was the imprint of long fingers, the touch of hard palms.

The shreds of nightmare faded as realisation hit. Jacqui's eyes snapped open on a pulse of shock.

She wasn't alone.

Ebony eyes, deep set beneath slashing straight brows, met hers. They were so intent, so piercing, she saw nothing else as she gasped in astonishment.

A frown puckered his broad forehead and tiny lines clustered at the corners of his eyes, giving him the look of a man who spent time outdoors in the sun.

Jacqui blinked, unable to do more than digest the fact she was awake *with a total stranger*.

A stranger who transfixed her with his gleaming, dark gaze.

Yet even as she thought it a memory stirred, a hint of recognition. He seemed…familiar.

'You're all right now?' The concern in his voice was echoed in his scrutiny and the line of his compressed lips.

Or was that annoyance?

Muddled and disorientated from the nightmare, she nevertheless felt no fear, sensed no threat. Surely it had been his voice, that warm, deep rumble that had dragged her out of horror and back to reality? Hazily, she registered relief she wasn't alone in the dark.

Jacqui struggled to breathe deeply, gratefully dragging air into her lungs, anything to dispel the sharp, rusty tang of Imran's blood from her nostrils.

The man stood so close she inhaled the scent of his skin, like the deep notes of an expensive cologne, only real, not manufactured. It reminded her of exotic spice and hot, desert breezes.

His breath was warm on her brow and parted lips as she sucked in more air. Long lashes veiled his eyes as his gaze dropped to her mouth. Instantly heat shimmered across her skin and her bloodstream traced fire through her body as if someone had set a match to dry kindling. Her skin flushed and her bare breasts tightened.

Her reaction was so sudden, so shockingly unfamiliar, she simply stared back, stunned, her mind grappling to take in what it meant.

'Yes, thanks. I'm—' Awareness crashed upon her in a flurry of alarm. 'Naked!' she gasped, jack-knifing to sit up.

Dimly she was grateful he stepped back but her focus was on locating the cover she must have flung off. She *hoped* she'd flung it off. That it hadn't been dragged off her by a stranger.

Horror skated skeletal fingers down her spine as Jacqui grabbed for the lavishly embroidered throw that had slipped from the bed. She didn't *feel* like she'd been groped. She couldn't remember anything but the solid, calming warmth of broad hands on her shoulders. But how could she be sure?

Seconds later, with the cover wrapped tight around her over-heated body, she swung to face him.

Never turn your back on danger.

The stranger was tall, imposingly tall, which was saying something given her lanky height. Few men made her feel petite. The effect of powerful height was emphasised by the breadth of straight shoulders that filled the doorway. Jacqui's first impression was of hard, lean masculinity. Her second, that he hid something.

His expression was closed, almost stern, yet his gaze belied the sombre attitude. Those eyes looked heavy-lidded and secretive. They remained fixed on her face, thankfully not dropping to where she fumbled, tucking a stray edge of fabric under her arm.

She'd never experienced such an instantaneous physical reaction to any man. That unsettled her almost as much as finding him here, leaning over her.

Jacqui hitched the material higher and set her jaw, trying to control the apprehension tightening her flesh. Even the innocent brush of fabric against her skin seemed evocative, reminding her of her nakedness.

In all her years of travel she'd got packing down to a fine art. It was a sign of her distraction that for the first time ever she'd forgotten to pack her ancient sleep shirt. It hadn't mattered two hours ago, but then she hadn't expected to wake and discover a hero from an *Arabian Nights* fantasy towering over her. Or was he a villain?

'Who are you?' Her voice emerged faint and husky. She hated the tremor in it. She cleared her throat. 'What are you doing here?'

He didn't move yet she had the impression he stood taller, more imposing, if that were possible.

'I believe that's my line.' He paused, brows raised, as if waiting for her to answer.

But Jacqui had learned never to show weakness or doubt. She had a perfect right to be here and she refused to cower as if she'd done something wrong. He was the one who'd invaded her privacy!

Before she could tell him so, he spoke again.

'Who are you and what are you doing in my harem?'

CHAPTER TWO

HIS HAREM?

Jacqui's mouth sagged.

No wonder he'd looked familiar. Yet, in the photos she'd seen of Sultan Asim of Jazeer, his head had been covered.

Jacqui took in the thick, black hair that complemented the burnished bronze of his skin and threatened to flop over his brow. The media had dubbed him one of the world's most eligible bachelors. He had wealth, power and charisma. If the public ever saw him like this, bare-headed and slightly tousled in a way that amplified the potent sexuality of his strong, autocratic features, women would mob him wherever he went.

Though according to Imran plenty of women had already thrown themselves at His Royal Highness.

Imran.

Jacqui pressed a hand to her swooping stomach.

'You should sit.' It wasn't a suggestion but an order, cracking through the tension in the room.

Jacqui pushed back her shoulders and opened her mouth to tell him she was fine.

'The dream was disturbing. You shouldn't exert yourself yet.'

'You know about that?'

'Why do you think I'm here?' His lofty expression made a joke of her fear he might be a sexual predator. What would a man like Sultan Asim want with a woman as plain as Jacqui Fletcher?

Awkwardly, the long coverlet almost tripping her, she subsided on the bed. Silly, how weak her knees felt. But the dream had been so real.

'Are you all right?' He'd moved from the door but kept his distance. Clearly he had no desire to get close.

Grimly Jacqui acknowledged she wasn't in the same league as the sort of women rich, sexy potentates entertained. Nature had skimped on her curves, for a start. Was that why she accepted so easily that his interest wasn't personal?

'I'll be fine soon,' she lied. Experience told her it would take far longer to shake the miasma of that dream. She tugged the covering close.

'Do you get them often?'

Her head snapped up. What did he see as he scrutinised her so closely? Terror? Grief? Guilt?

Instinct urged her to protect her privacy. 'Occasionally.'

'You should see someone about them.'

'You seem awfully interested in my sleeping habits.'

Was that a flush of colour across his cheekbones or a trick of the multi-coloured light?

Jacqui tensed and rubbed her forehead; a headache was beginning. Nerves and stress made her snap at the man who had the power to make or break this venture.

How could she? Everything rode on the Sultan's goodwill.

She wished she could blame her stupidity on being disorientated after the nightmare. Yet Jacqui had an awful suspicion her reaction to the Sultan himself was to blame. He was just… too big, too masculine, too close, though he stood metres away. It was as if the spacious room had shrunk and couldn't accommodate the two of them.

'I'm sorry,' she murmured huskily. 'I apologise.'

'No need. I understand.' His voice was a deep burr that worked its way under her skin and turned her insides to mush. 'The circumstances are…unusual. I should apologise for breaching your privacy. Finding a stranger so close on waking must be disconcerting.'

No mention of her nudity, or his hands on her body.

Yet she had trouble thinking of anything else.

She should be relieved he clearly didn't want to be in her bedroom. What she'd thought was a gleam of sexual interest in those hooded eyes was nothing of the kind.

Yet for some reason tension still eddied between them.

'Now we've got the apologies out of the way…' he paused, as if waiting to be sure they had '…you can answer my question.'

'Your question?' Jacqui felt like a parrot, repeating the word, but her foggy brain was a mess of impressions. Imran. The barely familiar room. The shock of meeting the Sultan. The curious ripple of reaction deep inside when those dark eyes rested on her.

He folded his arms and Jacqui was momentarily distracted as the movement moulded his long robe to a body that was even larger and more powerful than she'd imagined.

'Exactly who are you?'

Amber. Her eyes were a luminous shade of amber. A warm, enticing shade that made him think of sunrise over the desert, or the peachy reflection of late-afternoon light in the pool at his favourite oasis.

Asim had been stunned by that glowing brightness when she'd looked up at him. Those wide-spaced, slightly slanted eyes gave her an intriguing feline look.

He found himself staring.

Better staring at her eyes than her naked flesh, his conscience taunted. He was the lion of Jazeer, ruler, law-giver and leader. He did not ogle defenceless women.

Yet the image of her lithe, streamlined body had lodged in some unrepentant part of his brain and he couldn't shift it.

She hunched her bare shoulders and he realised he was scowling.

'I'm Jacqui Fletcher.' She sat straighter, meeting his eyes

directly, as few in his kingdom did. His pulse pounded as their gazes meshed. That was unprecedented.

Asim waited but she appeared to be pausing for his response. Was he supposed to know her? Something about the name rang a bell but he was sure they'd never met.

She understood his language, had responded in it, though she'd switched to English once she'd become aware of her nudity. Presumably shock had made her revert to her mother tongue.

'How do you come to be here?' His security staff had questions to answer. This section of the palace was well beyond the public audience rooms.

'I was invited.' Her head tipped up, though her gaze slid from his. Instantly he sensed she withheld something.

'Indeed?'

She flushed and Asim watched, fascinated, as colour washed her cheekbones and throat. With her tousled, tawny hair around her shoulders, flushed skin and flimsy covering, she looked alluring yet strangely innocent.

Damn! He needed to focus.

'I don't recall issuing any invitation.'

Again that lift of the chin, baring her slender throat. Did she realise how sexually provocative she looked with all that cream and rose flesh on display and her cover slipping low over her pert breasts?

'It was from the Lady Rania.'

'My grandmother?' What was the old schemer up to now, inviting strange women into the palace? Not just into the palace but deep into the long abandoned heart of it that hadn't been modernised in a century.

Asim sensed intrigue. He had an instinct for it, given the poisonous environment in which he'd grown up.

'Strange she didn't mention this invitation to me.'

A shrug drew his attention back to those bare shoulders, milk-white above the embroidered silk. A dart of heat jabbed low but Asim ignored it. He had more important issues to deal with than sexual awareness.

'Really? I wouldn't know.'

He told himself the husky, nervous voice proved she hid something. But his wayward body was too busy responding to the eroticism of that rough velvet tone.

Asim stood straighter, infuriated by his inability to focus. His day had turned to disaster because of one unwanted female. His night was rapidly going the same way. He fast lost patience.

'Why are you here, Ms Jacqui Fletcher?' A thread of memory tugged in his brain. He knew that name. 'You should be in a guest apartment near my grandmother.'

Something was going on behind his back and he didn't like it. He should have known when the old lady had been so uncharacteristically quiet this last week. His beloved grandmother was many things—opinionated, capable and clever—but never meek. He'd begun to worry she was unwell, that age and grief had finally caught up with her. He should have known better.

'I'm here to research a book. I'm a writer.'

Asim frowned. 'A writer?'

In a blast of realisation, it came to him. He knew where he'd heard of her. He froze, every nerve and sinew stiffening. Incredulity widened his eyes.

'Not Jacqui, but *Jacqueline* Fletcher. Am I right?' He watched her gulp and knew he wasn't mistaken. 'And not a writer, a journalist. Isn't that so?'

Anger spurted in his veins. What was the old woman thinking, bringing a journalist into their midst? Bad enough at any time but *now?* Sheer lunacy! They had too much to lose.

And this wasn't just any journalist. Anger turned to white-hot fury. She'd been there the day Imran died.

Asim drew in a searing breath, forcing back grief. His cousin had been on assignment with this woman. They'd headed out together for an interview. But only one had returned.

* * *

Jacqui clutched the fabric tighter at her chest. The silk kept slipping through her damp palms.

She'd planned to be fully dressed if she met the Sultan. She bit her lip, suppressing an insane urge to giggle. There was nothing remotely funny about this.

Sultan Asim had the power to scupper her project before it got off the ground. How could she convince him of her case, dressed in a bedspread and dazed from her nightmare? He'd never take her seriously.

Instinctively she rose, locking wobbly knees as she pushed the hair from her eyes.

'My by-line is always Jacqui Fletcher.'

'But you were identified as Jacqueline in the official reports.' Accusation rang in his tone and she flinched.

Jacqui knew the reports that he meant. Police reports, diplomatic reports, hospital and media updates. It was amazing the paperwork caused when two foreign news reporters got caught up in a supposed terrorist blast, even if it was in a distant African nation. She swallowed. It felt like broken glass lined her throat, scraping her raw.

'That's my given name but I never use it.'

'No.' His face turned to granite. 'I understand you prefer to be called Jack.'

Imran. Her fragile composure cracked. Imran must have mentioned that to his cousin.

'It's a nickname my colleagues use. Used.' She drew a shaky breath that didn't fill her lungs.

'You were my cousin's partner.' It was a statement, not a question, yet Jacqui had the impression he probed. Did he think them lovers? His gaze scoured so intently she felt it abrade her skin.

Remorse filled her. Here she was in Imran's childhood home, meeting his family, while he...

'We were colleagues, and friends.' He'd been the nearest

she'd had to a best friend. Her throat closed on a searing ball of emotion.

No wonder she'd thought this man familiar. He and Imran shared that superior nose and striking good looks. But, where Imran's eyes had danced with mischief, Jacqui couldn't imagine the Sultan laughing. His brand of handsome was harder than his cousin's. Those features looked like they'd been sculpted into proud, spare elegance by the desert winds.

'I'm sorry for your loss.' Her voice was hoarse. She'd written to Imran's family after he'd died but today was the first time she'd met any of them.

'Thank you.' He inclined his head in a gesture that was at once courtly yet distancing.

As if he didn't want her sympathy. He disapproved of her.

The knot of guilt in her stomach twisted tighter. She couldn't blame him. It was her fault Imran had died. If she hadn't dragged him to what had clearly been a set-up, he'd still be alive.

And she'd still be a journalist.

Brittle ice crackled in her veins and she hugged the bedding tighter. She desperately needed to be alone. But the man before her looked as immoveable as this massive ancient citadel.

Obviously her state of undress didn't faze him. She wished she could say the same. She was used to men, spent most of her time with them, but always fully clothed as one of the guys. Now she felt hyper-aware of her femininity and her nakedness.

'My grandmother invited you *here* to research a book?' Disbelief dripped from every syllable and his sable eyebrows shot up.

'She did.' Jacqui scrabbled for poise. How she wished she wore her charcoal trouser suit, or even the wrinkled cargo pants and long sleeved T-shirt she'd travelled in. Something familiar that would boost her confidence in the face of his imperious disbelief.

Once she'd have taken it in her stride, a challenge to be overcome to reach the next professional goal. But that certainty had been blown apart the day the bomb had exploded. She felt battered and unsure of herself. It wasn't just the trauma of the dream and waking to his disturbing presence. These past months had taken a terrible toll, not only on her career, but her confidence.

She wasn't the woman she'd been.

The realisation stiffened her spine. Hadn't she determined to drag herself out of the dark void of despair and fear? Hadn't she promised she'd make a success of this?

After all, it was all she had left.

She *had* to succeed.

'The Lady Rania was very supportive, and *hospitable*,' she added with deliberate emphasis, ignoring the whisper of her conscience that he had a right to resent her presence. 'She personally invited me to stay here—' her gesture took in the muted beauty of the ancient room '—in the heart of the old palace.' Jacqui forced a smile, as if she couldn't read the Sultan's disbelief. 'I'm most grateful to her.'

His expression grew more brooding.

'Clearly you can't remain.'

Jacqui's smile died. 'But I—'

He gestured in a slashing motion that signified no argument would be brooked. 'This is no place for a guest.'

Jacqui put her palm to her chest where her heart crashed into her ribs. For a moment she thought he'd meant to evict her from the royal residence. That would have been disastrous, the end of all her hopes and plans.

Relief eased the rapid beat of her heart.

'I'm perfectly comfortable, truly.' After some of the places she'd bunked down, this was luxurious, despite the lack of modern facilities.

Again his brows rose. Yet it was true. Besides, the tranquillity here soothed after the bustle of the capital. Even now, months after the explosion, Jacqui was edgy and uncomfortable with crowds or sudden noise.

'Nevertheless, it's not appropriate.' He looked as if he'd

swallowed something sour. It hit her that he might be talking about more than the lack of amenities. Did he think she was going to filch the silver? His stare was disapproving.

Strange how that hurt, though she should have expected it. He clearly blamed her for what had happened to Imran.

But the Sultan's grandmother had been so supportive and kind, first via correspondence and then today in person, that Jacqui had believed she'd be accepted here. She'd let herself believe that in completing the project she and Imran had discussed she could somehow atone for what had happened. Was that even possible?

'I'll have someone move you to another room.' He inclined his head and turned away.

Jacqui's old spirit surfaced. Being dismissed had always rankled.

'That's very thoughtful of you, Your Highness.' She grimaced. It was too late for royal protocol—the man had already seen her naked and screaming her lungs out—yet surely it couldn't hurt. 'Truly, there's no need. I'm just so grateful to the Lady Rania for allowing me such access.'

He stopped in his tracks, his neck and shoulders stiffening. Was he so unused to anyone speaking up once he'd dismissed them?

Imran hadn't talked of his cousin much, apart from occasional references to his focus on duty and royal responsibilities. The man had none of Imran's laughing charm. She guessed he was too self-important to bother charming anyone.

Slowly he turned. His face was impassive, but those night-dark eyes glittered sharply. Jacqui sucked in a breath and fumbled for a better hold on her covering as her fingers momentarily slackened.

Silently she cursed her misfortune in being caught at anything but her professional best. But regret couldn't distract her from the way her body sizzled under his scrutiny. As if he was seeing her naked again.

As if she *wanted* him to!

Abruptly she looked away, stunned. What was happening to her? She didn't react like this to any man. She closed her eyes momentarily, wishing she could wake and find this was all just an extension of her nightmare.

'As you say, Lady Rania is very generous.' He paused as if to let that sink in. 'And I'm sure you'll find a guest suite more than adequate.'

'But...' Jacqui bit the inside of her cheek in rising frustration. Words were her trade. Why couldn't she summon the right ones now she needed them? Had she lost that too, along with her nerve and her best friend?

'Your Highness, it's the private part of the palace I want to research. Not the public function-rooms.' She dredged up what she hoped was a winning smile and forced herself to meet his eyes. 'I'm writing about the women of the palace and their lives here.'

Obviously she'd lost her touch. Far from being persuaded, Sultan Asim's face turned stony. His lips thinned, his nostrils flared and his hand slid to a jewel-encrusted scabbard she hadn't noticed at his side.

Instinctively Jacqui stepped back as the man in the flowing robes transformed from autocrat to warrior in the blink of an eye. He looked dangerous and magnificent. As if he was on a raid into enemy territory.

Except he looked at *her* as if she was the enemy.

Her nape prickled and her breathing shallowed. Instinct told her to run. Her heart hammered.

Surely that curved knife was for show? Sultan Asim was renowned for diplomacy and leadership, not violence. Nevertheless she crept a little further away.

'You intend to write about the women of the palace? And my grandmother *agreed*?' His voice was a bass rumble that made her skin ripple.

Jacqui planted her feet, refusing to back up again. 'She not only agreed, she was enthusiastic.'

What was his problem? He hadn't looked this menacing even when they'd spoken of Imran. This was about something else.

'I find that difficult to believe.' He shook his head, folding his arms across his wide chest. The light of battle disappeared from his eyes, replaced by condescension as he looked down that sexy, arrogant nose of his.

'I assure you, Your Highness, I'm not in the habit of lying.' Anger took her across the room till she stood only an arm's length away. He might be lord of all he surveyed but that didn't give him the right to call her a liar.

She breathed deep then regretted it as she inhaled the hot, enticing scent of his skin. It infuriated her that she noticed it. She fixed her gaze on his face and ignored the predatory glint she saw there. This time, instead of frightening her, it spurred her on.

'When I told your grandmother I wanted to write about the traditions of the harem, she was enthusiastic. That way of life has disappeared and I want to document it.'

'You want to write about women from the *past*?'

'That's what I said.' Jacqui frowned. 'The women of the palace and their lives here. Or perhaps you think women's stories aren't important?' The challenge slid out before she could stop it. She was on a roll, too keyed up to pull back, though she knew she should.

Maybe because living dangerously was far more appealing than the dark nothingness she'd inhabited these past months.

Tonight, for the first time in ages, she felt blood pump in her veins. She felt *alive*.

'History is about more than wars and politics and who runs the country. What happens on a domestic level is important too.'

'Yet you made your name chasing stories about wars and politics and who run countries across the globe.'

Jacqui blinked, rocked by the fact he knew about her career. And by the reminder of all she'd lost.

'I'm interested in a lot of things. My background in news journalism doesn't mean I can't branch into something different.'

At least she hoped it didn't. Nerves made her stomach clench and her palms dampen.

She didn't know yet if she had what it took to make this dream a reality. But it was the only dream left to her. She'd cling to it with both hands. She owed it to her friend and to herself.

The Sultan surveyed her silently, as if she were a curiosity. Because no one ever stood up to him? She was pretty sure royal protocol didn't allow for contradicting the sovereign.

Jacqui drew a shaky breath and prayed she hadn't blown her one chance. She *couldn't* fail before she'd even started.

'Your grandmother is one of the few people who remember such a life here. She's a valuable resource and it would be criminal not to record what she remembers. This is part of Jazeer's culture and history.'

'You're very passionate about this.'

'There's nothing wrong with being passionate about what you do.'

Unless it leads you and your friends into danger.

Unless it destroys lives.

Memory was a sucker-punch to the belly. Her shoulders hunched, the pain almost doubling her over. Here she was, arguing trifles when Imran would never again feel the sun on his face or see his family. Because *she* had led him into danger. Maybe it was only just that she'd lost her career, her old life, as a result. Maybe she deserved to.

A firm hand closed around her upper arm, holding her steady.

'Slow breaths.'

Jacqui closed her eyes and nodded, focusing on breathing out through the pain.

The heat of his big frame radiated against her, counteracting the chill deep in her bones. The reassurance of his grip seeped strength into limbs that had turned limp.

'Here,' he said. 'You'll feel better if you sit.'

Jacqui opened her eyes as he led her to the bed. She almost sighed out loud with relief as she sank onto it. Immediately he withdrew his hand.

'Thank you,' she whispered. 'You're very kind.'

'You shouldn't exert yourself. You were distressed earlier and that took a toll.'

Dully, she nodded. 'I'm…' She shook her head.

What could she say? *I'm a mess right now* might be the truth but she had just enough pride left not to blurt that out. Though after the last half-hour baring herself to this man physically and emotionally she didn't have much dignity left.

'What's so funny?'

Jacqui lifted her face to find him a mere step away, a frown marking that broad, handsome brow.

She bit down a half-hysterical laugh.

'Just myself.'

If she didn't laugh she'd curl up in a ball and sob. She'd probably blown her chance to work on this wonderful project. It had shone like a beacon, dragging her out of the inertia of despair and fear.

'Can you dress yourself?'

Jacqui blinked. Was he offering to do it for her? Her over-tired brain boggled.

'Of course.'

'Good. Be dressed and ready to move in ten minutes.' Having given the order, he spun on his heel and strode out of the room, only pausing to be sure the door snicked shut behind him.

CHAPTER THREE

ASIM PACED THE COURTYARD, resolutely dragging his mind from imagining Jacqueline Fletcher discarding her less than adequate covering.

She was an enigma. Passionate and argumentative, not knowing when to give up. Fiery yet vulnerable. That made him want to ignore the danger she represented.

His desire to protect her was equalled by a burning desire of another kind and that was unnerving.

Yet he wanted to blame her for being alive when Imran wasn't.

He spun on his heel.

What was his grandmother thinking, inviting a *journalist* here? Having a professional snoop under the same roof—no matter how large a roof—invited trouble. Any further invasion of his sister Samira's privacy could tip her into a complete breakdown. The doctors hadn't said it outright but it was what they feared.

His stomach knotted. Samira had endured so much because he'd failed to protect her. The knowledge ate at him like acid.

Reluctantly he'd supported her plan to study overseas, only to learn she'd embarked on a passionate affair with a Hollywood actor who was the epitome of shallow self-absorption. But Samira had had stars in her eyes, had talked of marriage and hadn't seen him for what he was.

She'd only found out when he'd been discovered in bed

with his co-star by the woman's wrathful husband. Acrimonious divorce proceedings had ensued, eagerly reported by the press. Scandal grew with stories of multiple infidelities, drug use and even the corruption of minors.

Samira was an innocent party in the morass of stomach-turning revelations about her boyfriend and his co-star. But the press didn't let up. Once the darling of the paparazzi with her stunning looks, aristocratic heritage and high-profile romance, now she was their prey.

She'd sought refuge here. Only he and his grandmother and a few select staff knew that, as well as being heartbroken, Samira had to recuperate physically too. *That* story would never make it into the press.

He'd never known fear such as he'd experienced when he'd thought he might lose her. He'd felt so ineffectual. But this, now, was a situation he could control.

Asim grimaced, raking his fingers through his hair. He'd do whatever it took to keep his little sister safe. He wouldn't fail her again.

Had Jacqueline Fletcher told the truth about writing a book? Or was it a ploy to get a scoop on Samira?

Suspicion ran deep in Asim. How could it not after he'd witnessed the web of lies that had been his parents' marriage? How could he trust the woman who'd been caught up in Imran's death?

Yet he couldn't get a handle on her. He knew she was a respected news reporter. She was Australian, though she'd spent years in Africa, Asia and the Middle East. He knew she'd been with Imran when he died.

Everything else was speculation.

Speculation and an unhealthy dollop of attraction.

Asim shook his head, fed up with his circling thoughts. It was time.

He knocked but didn't enter. Better to be sure she was decently covered. The door swung inwards.

'You!' Those stunning eyes widened and it struck him again how fragile she looked. Was that real or some trick?

Asim stepped inside and she shifted back.

'Sorry,' she murmured. 'You surprised me. I expected one of the servants.'

Is that why she was dressed in drab trousers and a navy top that leached the colour from her face? She wore no make-up and had pulled her hair back in a ponytail.

And still arousal beat low in his belly.

He frowned. Just because he'd seen this woman naked didn't mean he was going to have her in his bed, no matter what his body wanted. He had more sense than to hook up with a journalist. After what had happened to Samira, how could he? Besides, his women were always poised, polished and beautifully dressed, at least to begin with.

Jacqueline Fletcher was…no; not ordinary. Not with those eyes or that mouth. But nor was she sophisticated.

'It's after one a.m. Why wake someone when I can lead the way?' Besides, he intended to keep a personal eye on her.

He scanned the neatly made bed then picked up the single suitcase and laptop bag. She travelled light. His sister had arrived with more than half a dozen cases, probably full of shoes. 'Is this all?'

'Yes, but I'll take the laptop.' She reached out but at a look from him her arm fell.

Why so eager to take the computer? Because she had something there she didn't want him to see or simply a journalist's instinct to protect the tool of her trade? Suspicion stirred anew.

'I can just about manage them both.' He nodded to the door. 'After you.'

She moved with a grace that belied tiredness or nerves. Baggy trousers hid her slender curves but his mind filled the blanks.

Asim turned off the lamp and followed. In the dim corridor it took a moment for his eyes to adjust but he sensed when he reached her. His nostrils twitched as the sweet tang of her perfume reached him. Something fruity and light that made him think of summer.

'I'll lead. Just watch your step. The old tiles are uneven.'

Silently she fell into step.

His mouth quirked. Who'd have thought this woman could be so biddable?

On the other hand, there'd been something curiously refreshing about the way she'd continued to argue her case after he'd stated his decision. Maybe Imran had been right and he was too used to getting his own way now he'd been Sultan so long.

His cousin had liked her, he recalled with a pang that crushed his smile.

'Where are we going?' Her long legs stretched to match his stride. Automatically he eased his pace.

'To a guest apartment where you won't be disturbed.' More to the point, she wouldn't have a chance to disturb anyone else.

'I'm very grateful for you taking the time to see me settled.' She was like a prim little girl reciting polite words she'd been taught.

If only she knew. Asim took her personally to her new accommodation because he didn't trust her. As soon as he had her installed he'd call security to ensure she didn't indulge in any night-time prowling. He refused to compromise Samira's safety.

'Is it in a modern part of the palace?'

'Yes, completed in the last ten years.' When he'd become ruler his one indulgence had been to build a suite of modern rooms for his own use and that of his private guests. The apartments his parents had used were too full of memories he'd rather forget.

'That will be…nice.'

Asim shot her a glance. 'They're very comfortable.'

'I'm sure they are.' She didn't sound enthused.

'But? There's a "but" in there.'

'Of course not.' He waited. Finally she added, 'It's just that I barely had time to explore the old rooms and they were so beautiful. That wall painting, for instance, with the climbing roses and the birds. It was magnificent.'

Curiosity stirred. 'You would like to stay in a place like that? Beautiful but cut off from the world?' It wasn't what he expected.

Moonlight lit her features as they passed through another courtyard. She looked serious, as if considering. 'It has a certain appeal. I'd enjoy it…for a while. But I'm a modern woman. Seclusion would lose its charm and I'd end up feeling trapped with nothing to do.'

'The women who lived there kept busy.'

She turned. 'Pleasing the Sultan? Being available to meet his every need?'

Despite himself Asim's lips twitched. She sounded almost prudish as she skated over the issue of sex.

'You've been reading too much fiction. It wasn't just the lord's wife or lover who lived there, but all his female relatives.'

He gestured for her to precede him into a corridor illuminated by glowing wall lights. Modern marble flooring replaced worn tiles underfoot.

'According to family tradition, that's why my ancestors were so warlike and successful in battle. It gave them an outlet for their frustrations since their female relatives tried to rule the roost at home.'

She slowed and he stopped, turning. Pale before, her face was animated now, delicate colour highlighting regular features. Even her lips looked plumper, rosier.

'There are two sides to every truth. I bet your male ancestors wouldn't have given up the freedom to ride across their kingdom, pick fights with their neighbours and grow rich from trade and war even if it meant living a life of domestic bliss. And as for the right to take the most beautiful girl in the kingdom as their own—'

Asim raised his hand. 'I see you've done your homework.' He shrugged. 'What can I say? Men will be men.' In his family, particularly so. Marauders, warriors and rulers, they had a reputation for fierceness as well as for honour and their impeccable taste in women.

He looked down into wide, seductive eyes and for an instant knew sharp regret that those old days had gone. A hundred years ago he'd have been within his rights to clap an intrusive journalist in irons rather than risk her reporting private family matters.

But he wouldn't have kept Jacqueline Fletcher in a dungeon. He'd have had her in one of those rooms adorned with murals of paradise. The bonds around her wrists would have been silk...

Suddenly she stepped back, her expression wary, as if she read his mind.

Asim blinked and refocused, stunned at his thoughts.

'Not far now,' he murmured, leading the way again.

What had come over him? He'd seen his share of naked women. Some would say more than his share. In his youth sex had been one of his favourite things. It still was, but these past months he'd exercised abstinence, distracted by Samira's problems and the need to finalise the agreement that had been signed tonight.

Maybe that was the problem. Once he'd have celebrated such a significant coup in the arms of a delectable woman. Instead he found himself guarding an unwanted intruder. An intruder with none of the glamorous allure he was used to, yet who provoked lurid thoughts of her naked and responsive in his bed.

He opened the tall entrance door to the Sultan's apartments.

He'd keep Jacqueline Fletcher from his sister. If she decided to wander she'd have to get past him first then his guards. Besides, he couldn't have left her far from anyone after that nightmare. Its trauma had been obvious.

Asim remembered Samira's frantic nightmares years ago when their parents' love-hate relationship had see-sawed violently. After screaming rows and smashing china, was it any wonder his kid sister had had bad dreams? She'd been weak and frightened afterwards.

No, he was doing the right thing, securing this woman close.

'This way.' He walked through the atrium and into a colonnade that ran beside his favourite courtyard.

'This is stunning.' She stopped to stare. 'Absolutely breathtaking.'

Asim followed her gaze. Trees offered shade during the day and the end of the courtyard was taken up by a long swimming pool, illuminated by underwater lights that showed off its aquamarine tiles. Concealed lighting above emphasised the decoratively carved arches of the colonnade, lending a traditional air.

'I'm glad you approve. I had a hand in the design.'

He ushered her through a door into a private sitting room. 'Oh my. It's…'

Asim strode ahead into the bedroom and put her case down. 'Too modern?'

He turned to find her standing in the middle of the room, eyes alight and a hint of a curve on her lips.

His pulse quickened. What effect would a full-blown smile have? He killed the thought, feeling as if it was a betrayal of his cousin.

She shook her head, turning to take in the airy space and the filmy curtains at the windows and pulled back from the bed. 'Absolutely not. It's sumptuous and gorgeous yet comfortable.' Abruptly she fixed him with that disturbingly direct look. 'It doesn't feel like a guest suite.'

Asim shrugged. 'That's what it's designed for.' He didn't add that only his intimates stayed here, one or two close friends and a handful of lovers.

Instantly he imagined her writhing naked on this bed…and she wasn't alone.

Abruptly he gestured to the bathroom, disturbed at the way his mind strayed around her. 'You'll find all you need. If not, call housekeeping. There's a phone beside the bed.' He spun away. 'I'll wish you a good night.'

'Wait!' Her voice came from close on his heels. He turned and there she was, within touching distance.

Clearly he *was* getting too used to being treated with royal distinction. Her nearness surprised him. Outside his family no one but a lover got this close without permission.

A buzz of anticipation filled him. Is that what he wanted from this woman? It was a lunatic idea yet his body's response told its own story.

'You've got my laptop.' She reached but stopped short of grabbing it from under his arm.

For a moment Asim considered refusing to return it. He could search it for anything she'd written about Samira.

Only for a moment. Such an act was beneath him.

Besides, anything she'd written could be rewritten and was probably already saved elsewhere.

With a slight bow he extended the case. 'What would a journalist be without a computer?'

She opened her mouth as if to contradict him then snapped it shut. 'Thank you. And thank you for your hospitality. The rooms are marvellous. I feel very privileged to be able to stay in the palace while I research.'

Asim shook his head, watching dismay tighten her features. 'Enjoy the accommodation but don't thank me so soon, Ms Fletcher. You'll be leaving tomorrow.'

He left before her inevitable protest. Yet he was surprised she didn't scurry after him.

He carried the image of her hurt eyes until he finally slept. Then he dreamed of a slim, pale-skinned woman laid out on his bed, awaiting his pleasure. Her hair was the tawny colour of the Jazeeri lion for which the country was famous and her voice husky as she pleaded for him to do all the things his burning body desired.

Asim paced his grandmother's sitting room. He'd slept badly and dealing with the Emir and his precious niece this morning had sapped his patience. He'd walked a razor-sharp line between hospitality and discretion and hadn't relaxed until he'd finally farewelled his guests. The assembled crowd's gaze had been like a dagger between his shoulders every time he'd even looked at the woman. She, devil take her, had cast him sultry looks and leaned close whenever they spoke.

He sighed and propped one arm on the window embrasure. It was a relief to have the woman out of his palace.

Now he just had one more female to eject.

If only his grandmother wasn't so obstinate about keeping her.

'It won't work. It's naïve to think she can remain if we want to protect Samira.' This time he'd keep her safe, keep control of the situation.

'Of course it will work. I'll see to it. They'll be in separate parts of the palace complex and Ms Fletcher will be busy with her research. She strikes me as a woman of considerable focus.'

Asim looked at the little dumpling of a woman from whom, he suspected, he'd inherited his determination. He wished she'd been here in the palace during his boyhood. She'd have been a welcome addition to their unstable household with her brisk common sense and kind heart. But his mother hadn't taken to her so despite centuries of custom his grandmother had retired to a summer palace in the foothills.

Yet for once Asim felt in sympathy with his departed mother. The Lady Rania, once fixed on an idea, was hard to budge.

He pinched the bridge of his nose, summoning patience.

'It's a recipe for disaster, putting a journalist under the same roof as a beautiful princess who's on the run from the press.'

'Ms Fletcher isn't that sort of journalist. She's not interested in kiss and tell affairs. She's here for a *real* story. I told you about the book she wants to write.'

Yes, he'd heard about the book. The table near his grandmother just happened to be littered with articles Jacqueline Fletcher had published about women's lives in Africa and East Asia. Clearly the woman was a workaholic. Given her demanding news job, he wondered how she'd found time.

'You really think there's a difference between a "news" journalist and the paparazzi?' He couldn't believe her naivety. 'Let either one sniff a story and they'll be onto it in a flash. Right now, Samira is news.'

'Samira is always going to be news.' His grandmother folded her arms. 'With her wealth and looks it can't be avoided. It's a matter of managing that.'

'You think having that woman here will help her manage the fallout?' He couldn't believe what he heard.

His grandmother fixed him with a shrewd stare. 'I think the two matters are quite separate. I see no reason for you to be concerned. I've already had a security assessment done on Ms Fletcher.'

'You have?' So his grandmother hadn't been as blindly trusting as he'd thought.

She nodded. 'Her life's an open book, and most of the pages are about work.' She paused. 'This project is important to her. She wants very strongly to make it a success. She won't jeopardise that by biting the hand that feeds her.'

Asim choked back a comment about taking the money and running. The press would pay handsomely for candid snaps of his sister right now, and even more for an insider's story on her state of mind, true or not.

'But *why* write this book? She's used to the quick adrenalin fix and high profile of current affairs. Why walk away from that at just twenty-eight? She's on the way to big things.' He'd done more checking of his own last night. 'It's too convenient.'

'You're too concerned with conspiracy theories, Asim. She and I have corresponded for some time. Even before Imran…' The old lady sucked in a shuddering breath. Her fingers knotted in her lap. 'He'd suggested she contact me and I believe she views it as her duty to your cousin to see it through.'

'Duty?' Asim bit out. 'It's a little late for that now he's dead.'

His grandmother shook her head. 'You can't blame her for what happened. You read the reports. You know she was as much a victim as Imran.'

Reluctantly he nodded. Logic told him the old lady was right. But Jacqueline Fletcher's presence here still felt wrong.

Not to Lady Rania. 'How can I turn my back on her when it was the last thing Imran asked of me?'

Asim watched his grandmother battle tears and his gut clenched. In seconds the clever, feisty woman he loved was gone, replaced by a fragile, grieving old lady whose distress tore at him. He felt as if someone was slowly disembowelling him with a rusty spoon. She'd always seemed indomitable but his cousin's untimely death had aged her as not even the loss of her son and daughter-in-law had.

Imran's loss had shocked them all. But for his grandmother it was a blow from which Asim feared she'd never recover. Unless she had something else to focus on.

With a sigh, he sank onto the arm of her chair and covered her age-knotted hands. He knew he'd regret this.

'You really want Jacqueline Fletcher here?'

Her hands stilled. 'I promised Imran.'

In their family a promise was an unbreakable bond.

Imran and Jacqueline Fletcher. Just how close had they been? The question had taunted him through the long night.

Asim closed his eyes, thrusting aside the futile wish that his grandmother's peace of mind could be achieved through other means. The only way forward was to take control of the situation, however unpalatable, and mould it into what you wanted.

'And if she proves unworthy of your trust?'

'I may be getting on in years, Asim, but I'm not in my dotage.' The indignation in her tone was a relief. 'I'm still a good judge of character. And talent.' She gestured to the papers on the table. 'Read those and tell me she's not gifted. She's got a journalist's instinct for a story, but it's tempered with humanity and respect.'

'Respect?' It wasn't a word he associated with the press.

'Read them and see.'

To please his grandmother, he scooped the papers up. The last thing his crowded schedule permitted was leisure for reading.

'You'll let her stay?'

Reluctantly he inclined his head. 'Since you wish it.'

'You won't regret it, Asim.'

'I hope you're right.' He would permit no one to hurt either his sister or his emotionally fragile grandmother. If Jacqueline Fletcher crossed that line she'd answer to *him*.

Jacqui paced the antechamber. Sitting still wasn't an option. Her response to a problem was to resolve it quickly. Except the Sultan had been unavailable all day. One didn't simply interrupt a busy head of state, no matter how infuriating and high-handed his attitude.

'His Highness will see you now.'

Jacqui spun round to see a young man gesturing her towards an open door.

Her empty stomach clenched. This was it. Lady Rania had assured her this morning that she'd persuade her grandson. But, remembering his severe expression and the glint of honed steel in his eyes, Jackie wondered if anything would shift him when he'd made up his mind.

Once she'd have been sure she could persuade him, but her self-assurance had shattered, leaving her questioning her judgement in coming here.

Yet if Jacqui didn't have this project, what did she have? Her insides heaved as she fought panic.

'Thank you.' She straightened her jacket with clammy hands and entered.

Though she was prepared, the sight of the man standing near the vast desk made her breath catch. He was taller than she remembered and memory hadn't exaggerated the breadth of those shoulders. Or the keenness of that stare.

Briefly she wondered if she should curtsey but knew she couldn't carry it off. Besides—heat seared her—after he'd had an eyeful of her nude body last night it was a little late for such niceties.

'Good afternoon, Your Highness.' Her gaze took in his finery: a long grey tunic embroidered at the high collar and hem, worn over pale, loose trousers that tucked into boots. No dagger at his side this time, but he wore a neat white turban threaded with silver. He looked imposing, his spare features harsh.

'Ms Fletcher. Please sit.'

And let him tower over her?

'Thank you but I prefer to stand.'

'Fine. What I have to say won't take long.'

Jacqui's insides tumbled in a sickening corkscrew. She planted her feet in her low-heeled shoes and braced herself. She should have argued her case last night but she'd been swaying with exhaustion after twenty-four hours of travel and then the trauma of the nightmare.

He paced closer and she had to make a conscious effort not to retreat. His gaze pinioned her like a hunter marking his prey.

Atavistic fear quivered through her as he came close and she read something in his stare that wasn't simply disapproval or dismissal. Something made her remember the brush of the silk coverlet against her bare skin and the strange jittery sensation deep in her core. She swallowed hard.

'You're lucky to have such an advocate, Ms Fletcher.' He was so close his breath warmed her and his hot spicy scent teased her nose. 'My grandmother is very taken with you. So I've decided you can stay.'

It took Jacqui whole seconds to take it in. She goggled.

'I can?' A smile trembled on her lips but they were too stiff to curve properly. Relief was a swoop of sensation through her chest so strong it hurt. She'd been so sure he'd banish her from the palace, perhaps the country.

'You may.' There was no lightening in his expression. If anything, it sharpened. He leaned closer, looming so her pulse jumped. 'But I have conditions.'

Jacqui nodded, feeling the force of his disapproval. 'Yes?' Her voice was a scratch of sound.

'One, absolutely no photos without permission.'

'Of course. I—'

'Two, no attempt to report on my family's personal lives. A social history is one thing, digging for gossip is another. I won't hesitate to sue if necessary.'

Outrage stirred. 'That's not what I'm here for!'

Astonishingly his hand reached out to cup her chin, tilting it up till his face filled her vision. Tension snapped between them and an unfamiliar sensation shot through her as his fingers splayed over her throat, reinforcing her vulnerability to his superior strength.

No man had ever held her like that. Jacqui was torn between wide-eyed anxiety and a sudden, startling jab of excitement. She hated men who threw their weight around, who encroached on women. But as she arched back in his hold part of her thrilled at his masculine power.

She blinked. She must be going mad.

'My family is precious to me and I won't have them harmed.' He paused, his jaw tight. 'I've seen what damage the press can do.'

Slowly she nodded, surprised and a little daunted by this glimpse of the man behind the royal title. The man she was sure would bring retribution on anyone who hurt those for whom he cared. Curiosity stirred.

'Three.' He paused, his gaze flicking to her parted lips then to her eyes. To her dismay her mouth tingled from that look. 'You will sign a contract agreeing to these terms and I will meet with you regularly for updates on your progress. I intend to take a very personal interest in this book of yours.'

Jacqui swallowed. 'Of course.' She made to jerk her head away but his grip firmed. He didn't hurt her but the sensation of being at his mercy sent anxiety scudding through her, as it was meant to. Her jaw clenched. 'There's no need to assault me to make your point.'

'Assault?' His brows rose. 'I'm simply reminding you that while you're in my home, and in my country, my will is law. If you attempt to take advantage of my family you'll pay dearly. Understood?'

'I understand.' For a moment longer Jacqui stood unmoving. Then abruptly she slumped from the knees, her body weight dragging his arm down, pulling him off-balance. A twist, a jerk and she was free; another quick movement as he reached to support what he presumably thought was her fainting body and now it was she who gripped him, her thumb hard on the pressure point in his hand. His skin was firm and warm under hers.

Her chest pounded as adrenalin shot through her blood. She stifled a grin at the surprise in his coal-dark eyes. Suddenly, for the first time in months, she felt strong and confident. It was a heady relief after so long doubting herself.

'And I hope *you* understand, *Your Highness*, that I won't be intimidated.' Beneath her touch his pulse throbbed an infuriatingly even rhythm. 'If ever I want a man to touch me, I'll invite him.'

Slowly his mouth curved in a smile as lethal as a scimitar. 'I'll be sure to remember that, Ms Fletcher.'

Strangely, his words didn't reassure.

CHAPTER FOUR

'Is SHE ON your list of potential brides?' Asim's grandmother whispered as they stood side by side, farewelling guests from the formal reception.

He stiffened. He hadn't sought the old lady's help to find a wife but that didn't mean she wouldn't try to sway him.

'I'm keeping my options open,' he said as he watched the young woman in question leave with her parents. They'd loitered till the very end of the evening and he wondered if they'd hoped for some signal of preferment. If so they'd waited in vain. The girl was nice enough, but...

'She's very pretty,' his grandmother murmured. 'Very well brought-up.'

So well brought-up she'd barely spoken till Asim had asked her questions she had to give more than a 'yes' or 'no' answer to. Even then she'd kept her eyes downcast.

His gaze shifted to a knot of people so engrossed in conversation they hadn't realised the reception was breaking up. At its centre was a familiar tawny chestnut head. Jacqueline Fletcher, nodding at something one of the country's most renowned lawyers said. Even from here he saw the flash of her bright eyes. Asim couldn't imagine her standing meek and silent before a man her parents wanted her to marry.

His lips twisted in a grim smile as he remembered how she'd been anything but meek. She was too opinionated, too outspoken for comfort.

'And she's obviously eager to start a family.'

Startled, Asim turned to stare at his grandmother, only then realising she referred to the woman who'd just left.

'That's a definite plus,' the old lady murmured, 'Since you want heirs. Did you know she volunteers at the children's hospital? She adores children.'

'I'd noticed.' She'd only become animated when talking about children at the hospital and, blushing, about her hopes for a large family.

Asim liked children. He wanted his own. But he'd felt uncomfortable with a woman who seemed to have no interests beyond that.

'Her mother tells me she's an excellent cook. I suspect she'll be a wonderful home-maker.'

Asim arched an eyebrow and stared down at his grandmother. 'Why the hard sell? It's not as if I'm likely to starve for want of a good cook.' A wide gesture took in the remnants of the superb buffet supper prepared by the royal chefs.

'I'm just pointing out her good qualities. Why are you so touchy?'

He shrugged, frowning. Why *did* he feel dissatisfied? Tonight had been arranged so he could vet a potential bride in a setting which wouldn't make his interest obvious. Yet the result was strangely disappointing. 'I'm sorry. I thought I knew what I wanted and now I'm having second thoughts.'

She nodded. 'A man like you needs more than a sweet mouse, Asim, even if she is a domestic goddess. You need a real woman.'

He discovered his eyes were fixed again on Jacqueline Fletcher. He blinked as his grandmother's words sank in. A real woman.

But not one like his unwanted guest. So she could hold her own in conversation and had an enquiring mind. That was all. She didn't even dress to make the most of her assets. That dark suit would have been acceptable at a business meeting, but not tonight, where the women wore full-length gowns of impeccable quality.

Did she aim to draw attention to herself in some perverse way? Or did she think to hide herself behind the boxy cut of that jacket? Perhaps she'd worn it because of him. Did she really believe the unflattering style would make him forget her svelte, alluring body now he'd seen it laid out before him?

'Asim, dear. You're scowling.'

His jaw firmed and he stiffened as he realised his grandmother was right. He'd been Sultan for ten years, had been attending formal events since childhood. Concealing his thoughts in public was second nature. Until now.

'Allow me to escort you to your suite.' The deep voice was as rich and tempting as the thick Arabic coffee sweetened with wild honey that was a local specialty. It slid right through her insides, scorching as it went.

Jacqui swung round to find the Sultan beside her. Her pulse throbbed faster and an unsettling frisson pulled her skin taut. She'd been so busy saying goodnight to her new acquaintances she hadn't heard him approach.

All evening she'd kept her distance, though he drew her gaze constantly. A head taller than most of the glamorous crowd, he looked magnificent in pale trousers and a high-necked tunic of coppery gold that complemented the saturnine darkness and chiselled authority of his features. This time his turban was black.

Beside him she felt like a drab sparrow. For a fleeting moment she wished her travel wardrobe included something sexy and feminine, until reality punctured the illusion. She didn't own anything like that. Besides, she'd look ridiculous, a scarecrow pretending to be a fairy princess.

'Your Highness, thank you for the invitation to tonight's reception. You have such interesting guests.'

His dark gaze was impenetrable. She should be used to it. She saw it every day in his office when he subjected her to twenty minutes of questions and answers more gruelling than any editorial inquisition. Twenty minutes in which he assessed her with the intensity of a scientist viewing a lower life form.

And never once had she discovered the man behind the formal interrogation. She sensed a sharp intellect and decisive mind but there'd been few glimpses of the man she'd met that first night, the one whose quick distrust, kindness and latent sexuality had fascinated her.

Just as well. She didn't need that distraction.

'Had, Ms Fletcher. The evening is over.'

She looked around and realised he was right. The last scattered guests had left.

'Then I'll say goodnight too, Your Highness. Thank you again.'

'I'm glad you enjoyed yourself.' He fell into step beside her and she was inordinately conscious of his height and the swing of his arm close to hers as they exited the opulent room. He turned with her into the wide corridor away from the marble and gilt public rooms.

'Really, there's no need to see me to my door.'

'It's not out of my way.' He gestured for her to precede him under a stone archway decorated with carved calligraphy and semi-precious stones.

Reluctantly she stepped through. Those short daily interviews were unsettling enough. Walking empty corridors with him reminded her too strongly of that first night when he'd found her naked and screaming. He made her feel vulnerable, as if her defences had been scraped away like a layer of skin by the hot desert wind.

Or maybe it's because you're so aware of him as a man. A hot, sexy man.

His hand shot out and grabbed her elbow when she stumbled.

'I'm fine.' Jacqui made to tug out of his hold but found she couldn't.

His eyes weren't blank any more. What she saw there made

her breath quicken and sent a charge jolting to the apex of her thighs. Heat seared to the tips of her ears as she identified her body's reaction.

Arousal.

Jacqui swallowed over a throat lined with sandpaper.

For days she'd assured herself she'd imagined the throb of desire that first night. She'd focused on her work, interviewing Lady Rania and poring over documents. She'd kept her reports to her royal host businesslike. But in the dark of her solitary room each night she'd felt a rush of heat that made a liar of her.

Her breath quickened as he tilted his head, watching.

Then abruptly she was free, his strong fingers sliding away.

'Forgive me, Ms Fletcher. I realise you didn't invite that.' His lips curved in a wry smile that set her heart battering her ribs.

It took a moment to realise he referred to her defiant announcement that if she wanted his touch she'd invite it.

Suddenly Jacqui remembered the warmth of his skin on hers that first night. How his dangerous smile had undone something vital inside her. How, even when annoyed at his superior attitude, she was always *aware* of him.

'I should go. I have a busy day tomorrow.'

She turned into another corridor and infuriatingly he fell into step. He was so close she heard the faint swish of silks and linen as he strode beside her.

'So I understand. My grandmother is excited by the prospect of you meeting her old friends. I gather they're spending the afternoon with you, discussing harem life.'

'You know about that?' Jacqui hadn't told him in advance, suspecting he'd object to her spending time with women who were intimately acquainted with his family. He'd made it clear his family was off-limits. The discreet presence of a guard who trailed at a distance whenever she left her suite to meet Lady Rania or investigate the deserted harem constantly reminded her that she was here under sufferance.

If she hadn't been so engrossed by her research, or so

desperate to make a success of it, she'd have bridled at the surveillance. It made her smile grimly that, after the dangers of her old job, now she was relegated to pure desk work Sultan Asim felt he had to take precautions against *her*.

'My grandmother has spoken of little but this gathering.' He paused. 'Whatever comes of this project, I must thank you for bringing pleasure to her at a very difficult time.'

Jacqui's pace faltered. It was the last thing she'd expected to hear.

'I'm pleased you think so. But it's she who's helping me. Without her involvement this project wouldn't be possible. When Imran…' She cleared her throat. 'When your cousin mentioned the possibility of interviewing her I hardly dared hope she'd agree.'

'It's that important to you?'

She nodded. More than he could know. What had begun as an interesting idea for the future had become her lifeline, her only option. And one final homage to her friend.

'Please.' He gestured and Jacqui stared, discovering they'd reached the spacious courtyard outside her suite. 'Take a seat.' He led the way to a pair of comfortable looking chairs in the garden.

Jacqui hesitated. 'I really should—'

'I'd like to talk to you.' He stood, a commanding figure bathed in moonlight. It gleamed on the fine fabric of his clothes and turned his eyes to a dark glitter.

Instinct warned against a tête à tête in the darkness. But he was her host. She was indebted to him. She couldn't walk away.

Reluctantly she stepped from the lit passageway and took a seat, struggling to sit upright when the cushions invited her to lounge. He sat turned half towards her, half towards the long pool that shimmered invitingly.

Silence surrounded them.

'I'm curious,' he said at last. 'Why would a woman like you embark on this particular project?'

'A woman like me?' She strove to keep the indignation from her voice. What was he accusing her of now?

His reluctance to have her here, his hawk-like scrutiny of her research and her daily guard proved he didn't trust the press. But she'd hoped she'd allayed his concerns and he'd begun to trust her a little.

'I've read your profile, Ms Fletcher. You're one of Australia's youngest foreign news reporters and well regarded. You received an award for media excellence, though you were in hospital and missed the ceremony.' Jacqui tried and failed not to stiffen at the casual mention of the time when shock and guilt, as much as her injuries, had incapacitated her. 'You rarely take leave and when you do it's to follow another story. You have a reputation for doggedness and for grasping the bigger picture.'

'You've checked me out.' It shouldn't surprise her yet Jacqui sat straighter, nerves jangling.

'Of course. Don't pretend you haven't done the same.' Jacqui felt the challenge in his stare though his eyes were shadowed.

Finally she nodded. 'You inherited the crown at twenty-five. You were educated in France and England, including at the Royal Military Academy Sandhurst. You've got a Master's degree in business administration.' She paused, reflecting on those old reports of extreme sports and hard partying.

'Despite your early reputation for…adventure, since taking the throne you've gained a name as a broker in diplomatic and trade negotiations and as a leader of vision. You've built on your nation's loyalty to your family and are well respected.'

'*Touché*, Ms Fletcher.' Laughter threaded his voice, making it far too appealing.

Her fingers tightened on the arms of her chair. Sitting in the darkness with this man whose presence sent her senses into hyper-awareness was a supremely bad idea. Her nostrils twitched. She wished he'd doused himself in some expensive aftershave any man might buy. Instead, she guessed that far too appealing spice and man mix was innate to him.

'And so?'

'And so, after checking your credentials, I'm intrigued. Why step away from your career to write about a lifestyle that no longer exists?'

'I hope plenty of people will be interested in reading about life in a harem.'

'Because sex sells?'

He leaned towards her and she shifted back. 'The book won't be about sex.' She waved a hand. 'Or only in part.'

'But that's what readers will expect.'

Jacqui shrugged. 'I want to paint a portrait of a vanished way of life.'

'The question remains. Why give up a challenging, successful job for which you're receiving accolades to write this book?'

Her breathing hitched and when she swallowed it felt like she'd gulped a block of ice. It froze her from the inside. She tried to prise her fingers from their claw-like grip on the arms of the chair but couldn't.

He leaned closer. 'I'm surprised your network has given you time off for this. Surely they want you doing what you do best?'

Jacqui bit down a sour laugh. *What she did best.*

What she *used* to do best.

'I didn't take leave,' she admitted in a rush, the blood pounding in her ears. 'I resigned.'

Even now the admission dealt her a sickening blow. After years building her career it still stunned her that she'd actually walked away from the only thing that had given her purpose and identity—her work.

As long as she could remember she'd wanted to be a journalist. Now that part of her life was over and it was no more than she deserved. Because of her Imran had lost his life. The price she paid was small by comparison. Her shoulders inched high as tension radiated up from her clawed hands.

In the other chair her inquisitor sat comfortably, fingers steepled together.

'I see.' Something about his inflection suggested that, even if he didn't see the whole picture, he guessed most. The idea of him silently dissecting what she'd said pushed her into speech.

'I'm sure your grandmother has told you about the essays I've written.' She snatched a breath and hurried on. 'They were well received and I'd always thought one day I'd try my hand at a book.' Like when she retired.

'It's good sometimes to work on something longer term, without the quick demands of current affairs reporting.'

Except she'd thrived on pressure and deadlines. Being without them now created a new sort of pressure, increasing her fear that she wasn't cut out for this longer project. Was this all a huge mistake?

'And yet it's a remarkable decision for a woman with such a promising career,' he mused. 'To cut herself off from work which, from what my cousin used to say, was a vocation, not a job.'

Jacqui's breath hissed between her teeth. This man was too insightful.

'I assure you I'm devoting all my energies to this. I'm not playing at it.'

He waved his hand dismissively. 'But you must understand my doubts about this unlikely career choice. Especially when it coincides with heightened media interest in my sister's whereabouts.'

'You think I'm here to get a scoop on your sister?' Jacqui frowned. 'If that were so, surely I'd be staking out the private Caribbean island where she's staying?' That was where the pundits reckoned she was hiding, licking her wounds after a disastrous love affair.

Jacqui shook her head. Tunnel visioned as she'd been, she hadn't considered Princess Samira relevant. 'There was I thinking you doubted my qualifications. Or that I intended to write some titillating fiction about sex slaves rather than a well-researched history.'

'Both crossed my mind.' The admission was a slap in the face, making her skin tingle and igniting a spark of professional pride. 'But what I've gleaned from our daily interviews and my investigations has reassured me somewhat.'

'Somewhat!' Annoyance spiked. How disappointed he must have been when she'd reported on her research. So far she'd focused on marriage celebrations and the training of young girls in domestic skills like preparing the spectacular sweets for which the royal court was famous. Nothing at all salacious.

He shrugged casually, the movement drawing attention to those wide, straight shoulders. 'Your arrival just as Samira is being hounded by the press is too coincidental.' He paused. 'I've allowed you to remain for my grandmother's sake, but I can't be completely easy with your explanation.'

'You don't have much time for the press, do you?'

'My caution comes from experience.' His voice was steely.

Jacqui remembered the reports about his lovers and his jet-setting lifestyle before he'd inherited the throne. Even now he captured headlines wherever he went. The combination of stunning looks and extreme wealth guaranteed it. Then there were older reports she'd skimmed about his parents' volatile relationship. They'd provided perfect fodder for sensationalist media outlets with gossip about break-ups, lovers and jealous rages.

'I'm a journalist, not a paparazza!'

'So you tell me.'

Jacqui pursed her lips, thinking. He'd given her support… so far. But he could change his mind at any stage. Only one thing would convince him—the truth.

A shudder ripped through her and she hunched forward, her arms automatically crossing, holding tight, as if that could keep the pain at bay.

She could keep her secrets and hope he didn't change his mind about letting her stay. Or tell him what he wanted to know. Tell him what she'd not told a soul.

His patient silence, the sense of a listening presence in the anonymous darkness, won out. Or maybe she was just tired of hugging the truth to herself.

'Everything I told you is true.'

'But there's more.'

Yes, damn him. There was more. She sucked in a sustaining breath.

'I can't do that job any more. I've tried and…' She shook her head. 'I just can't.' Jacqui heard the wobble in her voice and bit her lip. 'I tried being in the field again and I just…shut down. I couldn't function. Even being in the newsroom, working at that end, with the bustle and the people and the pressure, it was too much.' She blinked and lifted her head to stare up at the clear, bright moon. She remembered staring at a moon like that from her lonely hospital bed that first night, when she still couldn't believe the horror she'd witnessed.

'Ever since the bombing, since Imran died, I haven't been able to work.'

'Post-traumatic stress?'

She lifted her shoulders in a tight movement. 'Trouble sleeping, trouble handling more than one task at a time.' It almost killed her to admit that. She'd been so proud of her professional skills. 'Trouble with loud noises and too many people.' On bad nights she couldn't even face darkness, fearing sleep and the nightmares it might bring. And beyond all that was guilt that she'd led Imran to his death. *She'd* been responsible.

'Tonight was the first night I've been able to stand being in a crowd of people without searching for suspicious packages or jumping at shadows.'

She told herself that was progress, but in some ways tonight had only made it all worse. For she'd spent the evening in conversation with such fascinating people, people she'd normally pursue for an interview. She'd had an idea for a report on current regional trade negotiations, but the thought of following it through had made her queasy. She'd been second-guessing herself, wondering if the idea was as good as she believed or if her judgement was flawed.

Forcing herself to face him, she laid herself bare, ignoring the shrieks of her ragged pride.

'I *need* this project. Once I realised I couldn't go back I had nothing. No job, no hope for the future. Until your grand-mother and I corresponded again after...Imran.' Jacqui swallowed over the obstruction in her throat and forced herself to continue. 'She was so enthusiastic, I realised the project was too big for the article I'd planned. It needed a book. So here I am.'

Jacqui didn't add that her work defined her. Relationships had never succeeded for her. She'd never belonged anywhere as she had in journalism. Burying herself in reporting, building a life around her professional goals was all she had.

Moonlight silvered the strong lines of his face as he surveyed her.

Did he believe her or still think this was a conspiracy to uncover dirt on his sister? Had she bared her secret shame for nothing? Was he going to kick her out?

'Thank you for sharing the truth.' His voice was rich and slightly rough, like crushed velvet rubbing on bare skin. 'I suspect you haven't shared that with many.'

None. But she refused to tell him that.

Jacqui was an intensely private person, having learned to rely only on herself from the day her parents had split. It had been difficult, discovering at ten that neither of your parents loved you enough to want you full time. That you came a poor second to their new families. That you didn't belong except as an unpaid babysitter. But it had made her strong. She gave thanks now for that strength.

'I realise it was difficult for you.'

She nodded, her throat still closed.

'I'll continue to monitor your progress' He paused and she felt his scrutiny like a touch. 'But you've put my mind at rest for now.'

For now? What hoops did she have to jump through to win this man's approval?

Jacqui felt wrung out. She wasn't sure she had the stamina to go another round with the Sultan, no matter how desperate she was.

Abruptly he stood. 'Come, it's late. I've kept you from your bed.'

In the gloom he extended his arm and for an insane moment Jacqui thought he meant to accompany her to bed. A jagged slash of heat scorched her, resolving into an eddying pool of liquid warmth deep in her abdomen.

'In my country a handshake is a sign of trust.'

Reluctant despite the unlooked-for compliment, Jacqui reached out and took his hand. It was just as she remembered, firm, warm and strong.

Instead of the expected handshake he pulled her to her feet till they stood toe-to-toe, close enough for her to feel his breath on her forehead. The heat in her belly flared and sparked and a new kind of tension stirred.

There it was again, that searing stare that spoke of things far more intimate than news stories or remembered anguish. Breathlessly Jacqui told herself it was a trick of the moonlight that made his eyes glitter.

Yet instinct made her pull free of his hold. Not because of what she thought she saw there but because of the answering hunger growing inside, banishing the last glacial chill of memory.

She'd never known such an overwhelming response to a man. It made her want to run and hide.

'Good night.' She kept her head up, resisting the impulse to rub away the imprint of his touch. It was too unsettling but she knew better than to reveal that.

'Come, I'll see you to your door.'

'There's no need to go out of your way.' Her voice sounded scratchy and breathless and she cursed this sudden rush of hormones.

'It's not out of my way at all. Haven't you realised yet that you're staying in my private wing?'

Even in the darkness his slow smile packed a punch that made her reel.

'So if you need me in the night I'm not far away.'

CHAPTER FIVE

ASIM STARED ACROSS his desk at the woman before him, her head bent over her laptop.

Afternoon sun caught amber and russet tints in the hair she'd scraped back from her face. Idly he imagined it loose like it had been that first night, catching the light in a nimbus of gold and autumn hues.

He frowned. Blonde or brunette, or even tawny chestnut, no woman distracted him from his purpose.

His purpose was to protect Samira, no matter how tempted he was to believe Jacqueline Fletcher's tale of desperation. Yet hearing her voice catch as she'd told him why she'd begun this work, watching the moonlight silver a face pinched with pain, he'd wanted to comfort her.

Instinct told him her pain was real. But years of experience warned him never to trust a reporter. For too long they'd fed like jackals on his family. If he made a mistake trusting her when he shouldn't it would be Samira who'd suffer. The thought tightened every sinew.

Besides, Jacqueline Fletcher wasn't what she seemed. Her clothes were so drab and unfeminine it was suspicious, as if she aimed to deflect his attention but took the camouflage too far.

He'd seen her pearly skin, the flash of vivid amber eyes, the russet of pubic hair and the rose pink of her full-body blush. And he wasn't forgetting any time soon.

Heat doused him as she looked up. He felt wrong-footed,

as if caught ogling an innocent. An innocent whom his cousin had trusted.

'Here's the reference I wanted.' Her head tilted to one side as if she tried to read his expression and Asim stiffened as guilt eddied.

Instantly the shimmer of brightness in her eyes dulled and doubt jabbed him. Could she be such a good actress?

'Go on.'

She paused but didn't look away. Asim felt admiration stir. So often he merely had to hint at disapproval to find others giving way. Clearly his frown had no such impact on Ms Fletcher.

'It's a reference to diaries kept by...' she looked down to check her facts '...your great-great-aunt Zeinab.'

'And you found this where?' It was the first Asim had heard of royal diaries.

'There was a paper in the royal collection your grandmother thought would interest me. She arranged for your chief archivist to show me and it mentioned the diaries.'

'Tell me more.' This research project expanded before his eyes. First interviews with his grandmother, then visits to abandoned parts of the palace accompanied by various building experts, then meetings with an ever-expanding group of his grandmother's old friends. Now the royal archives. When would it stop?

So much for his hope he'd soon see the back of Jacqueline Fletcher.

'It mentioned arrangements to teach the ladies in the harem geometry, astronomy and poetry.'

Asim nodded. 'All are traditionally important to my people. Astronomy and geometry aid navigation in the desert and poetry is prized among all the arts.'

Again that tilt of her head. 'Yet the women of the palace weren't likely to navigate alone across the dunes.'

Asim shrugged. 'You think one should learn only the immediately practical? What about broadening the mind?'

'I agree.' Her gaze dipped. 'It just surprised me that your ancestors felt the same way, especially when it came to educating women.'

He repressed anger. Wasn't this the sort of too easy assumption many outsiders made? 'Despite the stories you've heard, many of my predecessors were enlightened. They sought beautiful, clever women as their consorts, women whose company they could enjoy. Educated women who could share their lives as well as their beds.'

'Which is why I'd like to access Zeinab's diaries. They will be invaluable—'

'No.' A journalist prying into intimate family details? Even after generations the diaries could reveal material better kept private.

'But if I could—'

'It seems to me you have plenty of sources already.'

He supressed a smile as her eyes flashed. No longer drab despite her dowdy clothes, Jacqueline Fletcher looked vibrantly alive with her flushed cheeks and pouting lips.

'The diaries will give a new perspective to the project, adding depth and texture.'

'I take your point, Ms Fletcher, but I prefer to keep such private material private.'

She met his gaze, her brow pleated.

Enough. Asim glanced at his watch. It was time for his next meeting. He pushed back his chair.

She stood, planting her palm on the desk and leaning forward. As if he were an equal, not an absolute ruler who'd already granted her great favour.

'Your Highness.' The way she said his title was anything but obsequious. 'Don't you see? This could be a chance to provide an insight into a woman who was both educated and well regarded. The diaries could provide material to refute the sort of assumption I just made.'

Asim paused. She had a point, damn it. If this book was to be written, better it be done properly.

'I'll consider the matter and discuss it with the head archivist.'

She shook her head, leaning in till the faint sweetness of her skin reached his nostrils. 'I talked to him and he...' she paused '...didn't see it as a priority.'

'Didn't he?' Asim could imagine it. The head of that department was a dry old stick who wouldn't have taken kindly to Jacqueline Fletcher's enthusiasm.

'No. But if you were to take a personal interest...'

Asim huffed out a laugh at her persistence, her sheer front. She didn't take no for an answer, no matter how demure she pretended to be. Sooner or later something would catch her interest and she'd light up in enthusiasm or outrage.

She was never dull.

'Very well.' He made a quick decision. 'I'll look at these diaries and, if appropriate, you will be allowed access under supervision.' His raised hand silenced her thanks. 'I understand that while you speak our language you can't read it fluently, so a staff member will translate any relevant sections.' A carefully picked curator who would protect the royal interests.

The radiance of her smile sent a trickle of heat through him and his mouth firmed.

Jacqueline Fletcher was convincing as an honest, dedicated writer rather than a conniving, duplicitous opportunist. But Asim wasn't completely sure yet.

The only thing he could be sure of was that his attraction to her was a complication he could do without.

If you need me in the night I'm not far away.

It had been days since the Sultan had said that but the words taunted Jacqui as she slid through the water.

Surely he hadn't intended it to sound so...intimate. As if he expected her to invite him into her bed. Yet the sizzle of elec-tricity between them was real. Even she could recognise desire.

Unless the sizzle was only *her* body's response to a potently masculine and charismatic man, not his response to her. Her mind and her body had let her down these past months. Had she imagined the sultry interest in his hooded eyes, projecting her own breathless awareness onto him?

Had he *really* brought her to his apartments in case she suf-fered night terrors? She spluttered, swallowing water.

She'd been so busy branding Sultan Asim high-handed, she'd disregarded the soft spot he'd shown for his grandmother and his protectiveness to his sister. He wasn't just an arrogant potentate. He knew how to care.

Could that caring extend to her? It seemed unlikely. Yet the alternative, that he desired her, was impossible.

Jacqui had no illusions about her sex appeal. She'd been a gawky tomboy, always playing sport with the boys. Puberty came late and no one noticed since her body had steadfastly refused to grow curves like other girls'. She'd simply stayed one of the boys. Not the sort of woman to attract a man like Sultan Asim with his renowned eye for beauty.

She remembered her few attempts in her teens to discover the secret of looking feminine. Her mum had pretended she was still a little girl and her stepmother, when forced to, had bought the same T-shirts and jeans for Jacqui as for her sons. She'd viewed Jacqui's occasional efforts to dress up as selfish attention seeking.

So Jacqui had taught herself with the help of hand-me-down magazines. The results had been spectacularly awful. There'd been no one to warn her that the pink frilly dress she'd spent all her savings on and the vibrant hot-pink lipstick made her look like a clown. Or a transvestite, as one of the little cats in her class had exclaimed.

By the time she was working Jacqui had learned the best she could achieve was neat professionalism and to avoid bright colours and clingy fabrics. Better to blend in than draw attention to her shortcomings.

A slamming door made her turn, treading water.

Late afternoon light slanted across the courtyard as a tall figure strode to the pool. Jacqui's eyes bulged and she almost forgot how to stay afloat until instinct shook her lax limbs into movement.

She'd thought him imposing fully dressed. But the Sultan of Jazeer had a body that looked even better without clothes. Almost without clothes. White swim shorts rode low on his hips, revealing acres of burnished skin.

Hot needles of excitement pricked Jacqui's flesh as she watched his easy, athletic lope. Those shoulders were even wider than she'd imagined, his body lean but well built. The dusting of dark hair across his chest emphasised the bunch of muscles as he moved.

She exhaled, trying to slow her racing pulse as she tracked the line of dark hair that arrowed down, plunging beneath his shorts.

Belatedly her brain engaged as she realised where she was staring. And that he watched her.

Jacqui struck out for the far edge of the pool, splashing in her haste.

She had sex on the brain, and it was the fault of Lady Rania and her friends. What had begun a few days ago as a small reference group of old ladies had grown with daughters, granddaughters and friends who saw their afternoon gatherings as an excuse for socialising. When Jacqui had asked about preparation for marriage in the harem, soon they'd been swapping stories that made her blush.

The art of pleasing a man sexually had been an essential part of a harem education. The trouble was now Jacqui's head was full of images of her trying those techniques on the Sultan's taut, powerful body!

Obviously she'd been cooped up here too long. She was having some weird harem fantasy.

At last she neared the edge and reached out, only to find him standing there, hands on hips, watching. Shock made her suck in a breath that turned out to be water and sent her under.

Spluttering, she grabbed for the rim of the pool. Instead of hard tiles she felt warm flesh. An instant later the water rushed by as he hauled her straight up and out of the pool. Jacqui found herself planted on her feet, his hands spanning her waist as she bent, coughing.

Was his touch hot or was that searing sensation her nerve endings going into overload?

Finally Jacqui blinked and straightened, hyper-aware of his hands encircling her middle. His long fingers made her waist seem tiny.

Her vision was filled with a broad chest that just asked to be touched and a squared-off jaw that proclaimed male power. She curled her hands into fists, fearing she might do something unforgiveable like reach out.

Yet when she made to shift away his hold firmed.

Shakily Jacqui pushed her sodden hair back and raised her face. Dark eyes surveyed her from under half-lowered lids.

That flagrantly carnal look seared her into silence. Her breath caught as his gaze dropped to her mouth. To Jacqui's horror she felt her nipples pebble as erotic energy zapped through her.

Why was he looking at *her* like that?

'Thank you, Your Highness. But I can stand without help.'

'Asim.'

'Sorry?' She stared at his mouth, not trusting her ears.

'I reserve the right to use first names with women I save from drowning, Jacqueline.'

The sound of her name in that deep, rich voice sent a quiver of excitement through her.

She was in deep trouble.

'I don't think that's necessary, Your Highness. Besides, I wasn't drowning.'

'Asim.' His fingers curled in, securing her, and she fought not to wriggle with pleasure. 'Say it.'

He looked every inch the arrogant prince with his austerely aristocratic features. His nostrils flared, his eyes narrowing to glittering obsidian shards.

Heaven help her, he was more powerfully attractive than any man she'd ever seen.

'Really, there's no need.'

His eyebrows rose loftily and there was steel beneath the velvet of his voice. 'You reject my offer of friendship?'

Asim looked at the woman in his hold and felt hunger rise, sharp and raw. She couldn't be trusted. She was a journalist, one of the breed that had feasted on the carcass of his parents' marriage and now preyed on his vulnerable sister. He'd be a fool to let her close.

Yet when he looked at her he saw simply a woman.

An infuriating, challenging, surprising woman who didn't know when to shut up or when simply to obey.

A woman who in her sleek, rust-brown one-piece swimsuit looked like a naiad. Water sluiced over her lithe frame, accentuating each streamlined curve and hollow. Her limbs glowed in the late-afternoon light, giving her a luminous quality that made her seem otherworldly.

Except the woman beneath his hands was real, so fine-boned his fingers almost spanned her waist.

But it wasn't her waist that drew his attention. His gaze fixed on her lips, pink and inviting.

'Asim,' she said finally in a throaty murmur that sounded more like invitation than capitulation and made his blood rush hot and hard.

'That's better.' His voice was a low growl and he heard her gasp.

He wanted to hear her gasp like that while she lay beneath him and he took them both to paradise.

Jacqueline Fletcher invaded his peace. Every day she visited his office to report progress. She was businesslike and brisk but those stunning slanted eyes would flare amber fire when something fascinated her. Then she'd forget her formality and her whole being would come alive with an enthusiasm Asim wanted to capture and taste.

Each day it grew harder to concentrate on her words or remember the need to be suspicious. He wanted to strip away her shapeless trousers and loose shirts and touch the pearly skin he remembered. His body tightened as he imagined her writhing in pleasure against him.

Except he was in the process of selecting a bride. He had no time for sexual diversions. Besides, honour dictated he shouldn't seek a mistress and a wife at the same time.

His brain said that. His body refused to listen. It told him a few hours' diversion was exactly what he needed.

Her teeth snagged on her bottom lip and he lifted one hand, pressing his thumb there, feeling her swift intake of breath.

'Don't. You'll draw blood.'

'Then let me go. I don't want this.'

Liar.

Asim was tempted to demonstrate how much she wanted precisely this. It would be easy to kiss her till she surrendered. He'd carry her to a bed and relieve them both of the pressure that had built inexorably since the night he'd found her naked in the harem.

'Please, Asim.'

Whether it was the fact she pleaded, this prickly, opinionated woman, or the way she said his name, in a voice barely concealing distress, Asim felt a fist lodge in his chest. Reluctantly he opened his hands and stepped back.

She looked up, those feline eyes gleaming with a slumbrous heat that made a mockery of her protest and his caution. Then he read the tension in her mouth. She'd paled, the tiny smattering of freckles across her creamy skin standing out like blood on parchment.

'I'm sorry I intruded.' She ducked her head and spun away. 'I should have realised you might want the pool.'

The fist in his chest twisted.

'Don't!'

Alarmed, she stared back over her shoulder.

'Don't apologise.' He breathed deep, filling the void in his lungs. 'I don't like it when you're...meek.' The words surprised him as much as her. He felt the shock of that admission reverberate through him, even as he saw it ripple across her face.

He didn't approve of the way she argued with him, refusing to be silenced after he'd made a decision. It happened daily when she tried to wheedle access to records or palace staff or ancient pavilions that had been locked up as unsafe generations ago. Yet seeing her hesitant and downcast was like watching a bright light dim.

For long seconds their eyes locked. Long enough for him to notice that in the syrupy late-afternoon light her eyes flashed with shards of gold.

Slowly her mouth eased into a crooked smile.

'In that case, Asim...' She paused over his name as if savouring it. 'I promise not to be meek with you again.'

She scooped up her towel and wrapped it around herself, hurrying towards her room. But her chin was up and her shoulders back and, despite his body's howl of protest at her departure, Asim found himself smiling.

CHAPTER SIX

'IT'S GORGEOUS, BUT I can't accept it.' Regretfully Jacqui tore her gaze from the liquid fall of pewter silk in her hand and turned to Lady Rania.

'Of course you can. You'll look marvellous.'

'It's kind of you but unnecessary. I'll wear my skirt and jacket to the dinner.' Seeing the other woman's raised brows, she hurried on. 'I'm here for business, not pleasure.'

Lady Rania shook her head. 'You have a lot to learn, Ms Fletcher. There is no reason why business cannot be spiced with pleasure, or why a lovely young woman cannot make the most of herself. After all,' she continued with a glance at Jacqui's long-sleeved top, 'The dress is modest.'

Jacqui didn't know how to respond. She couldn't admit she'd never worn a formal evening gown and had no wish to start. This slinky dress would highlight the deficiencies of her lanky frame. There'd be nowhere to hide in it.

Yet the slide of silk through her hand was seductive.

Jacqui wondered how it would feel, wearing this designer original against bare skin, and shivered. Maybe because her riotous imagination pictured strong, bronzed hands stripping it off her—Asim's hands.

Carefully she laid the dress over the exquisitely upholstered sofa. Everything in the dowager's apartments was delicate and feminine, everything Jacqui wasn't.

'It's just…' She wiped her palms down her trousers.

'Yes?' The old lady gestured for her to sit. 'You know it would give me immense pleasure to do this for you, Ms Fletcher. I don't think you realise how much your project has meant to me.' She smiled wistfully, a small hand gesture conveying a hint of frailness Jacqui had never noticed before. 'Everyone these days is interested in moving forward but never in looking back. It does an old woman good to be useful again. My friends and I have been useful, haven't we?'

'Absolutely.' Jacqui leaned forward. 'You've been a mine of information. My research would never have got off the ground without you.' She paused, wondering if the dress was meant as a farewell gift. Was this a signal her stay was about to end? 'I had hoped to continue working with you a little longer...'

Lady Rania smiled gently. 'I look forward to that. In the meantime, allow me to do this. Tonight will be a formal dinner and it would please me if you wore my gift.'

Put like that, Jacqui had no choice. 'Thank you.' She eyed the spectacular fabric and gulped. She could do this. She couldn't offend or disappoint the woman who'd been so good to her. 'I'm honoured by your gift.'

'Excellent.' Lady Rania sat straighter, that hint of frailty abruptly extinguished by her radiant smile.

Three hours later Jacqui took a deep breath and looked in the mirror.

She blinked and looked again.

That was *her*?

The woman in the mirror looked subtly elegant. Not ungainly or scrawny. A few weeks of eating the delicious palace food must have helped her put back on the weight she'd lost. She wasn't much of a cook at the best of times and in the months following Imran's death preparing meals had been too much bother.

Jacqui stroked her palms down the fragile silk covering her hips and thighs and felt a ripple of excitement glissade across her skin. She knew nothing about couture but even she recognised this had been styled by an expert. From the delicate drape of the cowl neck that made the most of her less than impressive bust, to the belt of silver metal links that cinched her waist and the full-length sweep of skirt, the dress was fabulous.

She twisted, frowning as she surveyed the narrow slit at the back of the bodice. It was just wide enough to prevent her wearing a bra. But what was the point of it when she was covered from neck to toe?

Swivelling back, she stared again. With her shoulder-length hair up in a deceptively casual knot that had required the expertise of Madame's personal attendant, and subtle make-up that enhanced her eyes and glossed her lips, she didn't look like boring old Jacqui Fletcher.

She recalled the way Asim called her Jacqueline in that slow, lilting way, as if he rolled the sound around his mouth. Did she look like a Jacqueline now?

She'd always thought it ironic her parents had chosen such a feminine name for a tomboy like her. Jack suited her better. But tonight… She cocked her head and a slow smile spread across her face. Trepidation gave way to excitement.

Tonight perhaps she had it in her to be Jacqueline for a few hours.

Asim dragged his attention back to the pretty brunette beside him. Her hands fluttered like tiny birds as she talked. Delicate colour flushed her cheeks and her eyes sparkled. The acid green of her halter-neck dress showed off her smooth olive skin to perfection and her glossy curls danced.

She laughed and without pause launched into another line of conversation. Asim's smile grew fixed.

No one could accuse her of being meek. She was talkative and friendly. Her trill of laughter turned heads and made their neighbours at the long dining table smile. Nor had she mentioned children. Instead of being fixated on babies her conversation ranged from the economy to her work in television and the latest reality television show, about which Asim now knew more than he wanted.

After two hours in her company he longed for silence.

Fortunately as Sultan there were many demands on his time. He and his wife need not live in each other's pockets. If he wished, he could avoid her easily.

After all, he didn't seek a love match. A shudder skipped down his spine at the thought. With his parents' example before him he knew any such relationship would turn destructive. That was the nature of love, at least in his family. He had no doubt he carried the same defective taint as his parents. Children of dysfunctional families usually did.

No, he didn't do love. He wanted a mother for his children and a helpmeet. She'd take her place at his side and share the burden of official entertaining.

Yet why saddle himself with a chatterbox, no matter how bright and cheerful? Asim wanted a woman who could hold her own in conversation but also knew when to hold her tongue.

Unbidden his gaze slid down the table to the svelte vision in silver that had robbed him of speech when she'd entered the room.

He stiffened, horrified at the way his attention kept straying there.

Jacqueline Fletcher wasn't the woman he sought. She didn't chatter, but she was more likely to question his decisions than support them. Right now she fielded the attention of two diplomats, a businessman and a cabinet minister who, rumour had it, was on the lookout for a new bride after a recent divorce.

Heat rippled under Asim's skin. She'd played him for a fool. All those weeks she'd covered herself up, he'd almost believed she was uncomfortable showing off her body.

Now she flaunted herself. With that clinging dress moulding her ripe breasts like a lover's caress, she might as well have worn a sign saying 'open to all offers'. And this after she'd pushed him away that day at the pool!

If she wanted to hook a man to enliven her stay, his royal dinner wasn't the place.

With a scowl he turned back to his companion.

'Where do you think you're going?'

Jacqui slammed to a halt, her hand going to her throat as that familiar, deep voice sounded behind her. To her horror, awareness unfurled in the pit of her stomach. If only she could conquer this response to him. But it grew worse, not better. She'd spent half the night snatching glances at him entertaining VIPs, among them a number of beautiful women.

Snagging a shallow breath, she turned and there he was, resplendent even in the low light of the quiet corridor, wearing a tunic of scarlet silk shot with silver, dark-grey trousers and a matching turban. All the other men tonight, even the handsome young diplomat who'd been so attentive, had faded into the background near Asim.

He stalked towards her, every inch the autocrat, his mouth a straight line, his look brooding.

'I repeat, where are you slinking off to, Ms Fletcher?'

'Slinking?' She stiffened. And *Ms Fletcher* when she'd finally got accustomed to Jacqueline? 'I'm not *slinking* anywhere.'

He halted less than an arm's length away, well inside her personal space. Jacqui frowned. Since that day at the pool he'd been scrupulous about maintaining his distance.

'No? Then why carry your shoes if not to be quiet?'

'They're new and they rubbed.' She'd felt like Cinderella leaving the ball, knowing the night's magic was over when she'd had to remove the sandals.

'But you've missed the way to your suite.' If anything his expression grew sterner. What was his problem?

'I wasn't going there.' She hadn't wanted the evening to end. Attending a royal banquet was an affair to remember. The company had been fascinating and she'd basked in the pleasure of knowing she looked almost pretty. She was too wired to sleep.

'You have an assignation?' Asim moved closer, his brow lowering. His expression made her shuffle back, disquiet rippling across her nerves. Suddenly the isolation of this rarely used corridor struck her.

'Assignation? No.' She stared squarely back at those dark eyes, indignation swelling. Was this about her supposedly digging up dirt on his sister? She'd thought they'd moved on from that.

'But this is the way to the rear gate of the palace.'

'It is?' She shrugged. 'It's also the way to the harem. I thought I'd sit in one of the garden courtyards for a while.' She'd avoided the one near her rooms ever since Asim had hauled her out of the pool and her body had gone into meltdown.

'Is there a problem, *Your Highness*?' She was sick of the way he stood there, glowering. She hadn't done anything wrong. She could have eaten her dinner with her fingers rather than the exquisite antique gold cutlery and he wouldn't have noticed; he'd been too busy gawping at the vivacious beauty at his side. 'If not, I'll go.' She moved past him, her happiness stupidly dashed by his hostility.

A hand snaked out, shackling her wrist and pulling her to a halt mid-step. Jacqui gasped. Even through the long, fitted sleeves his touch singed.

'What did you think you were doing, wearing *that* to the banquet?' His gaze scorched a trail from her neck to her breasts and lower, to where the silk flared over her hips before swirling to the floor.

The tone of his voice mixed anger with disapproval and for a moment hurt assailed her. Then she recalled Lady Rania's delight when she'd seen Jacqui in the dress, and the interest in her dinner companion's eyes.

'Dressing for dinner.' She bristled. It was on the tip of her tongue to tell him to take his bad mood and shove it, but he had the power to eject her from the palace. She drew a slow breath and pretended not to notice the way his gaze flickered on the movement. 'Your grandmother—'

'No!' He raised his free hand. 'Don't bring her into this. This is about why you chose to wear that—' he gestured disparagingly to her beautiful dress '—to an important royal occasion. You must have known the effect it would have.'

Jacqui stared up at him, seeing a flash of fury, and felt her eyes widen. He was serious. And he was mightily offended.

To her horror something crumbled a little inside. Could she have got it so wrong? Had Lady Rania been too polite to tell her she'd been mistaken about the gown suiting her? Had the diplomat's assiduous attention been too over-done? Could he have felt sorry for her, trying to masquerade as glamorous when she wasn't?

Jacqui swallowed and it felt like razor wire lodged in her throat. She'd never been a good judge of fashion. Had she been blinded by the beauty of the dress into thinking it could transform her with a mere slither of its silk?

A horrible churning sensation filled her insides. Normally she didn't worry too much about how she looked. But tonight she'd thought...

'It won't happen again, Your Highness.' Her voice was wooden but she refused to look away and let him see how much the truth hurt. 'Next time, if there *is* a next time, I'll wear my suit.'

He nodded stiffly. 'That would be preferable to making an exhibition of yourself.'

Jacqui tore her hand from his, anger and hurt spiralling uncontrollably. It was one thing to know her limitations after having her stepmother harp on them so often, but it was horrible to hear *him* spell them out.

'Damn you!' She snarled the syllables between gritted teeth. 'That's a horrible thing to say.' Her breath sawed in her throat as she strove for breath. 'We can't all be glamorous and sexy like you but that doesn't give you the right to belittle others for the way they look.'

Jacqui marched away, only to catch herself up on her long skirt. Cursing under her breath, she scrabbled at the slippery silk, lifting it enough to walk, and strode off.

She'd gone two steps when he grabbed her elbow and swung her round to face him.

CHAPTER SEVEN

'YOU'RE NOT SERIOUS.'

But those amber eyes spat fire at him. This was no joke. And there was hurt in the twist of her mouth.

His stomach dived.

'Never more so.' Her jaw angled so she could look down her nose at him, despite the fact he was so much taller. This woman had sass.

She also had sex appeal in spades. Only iron willpower kept his hand on her elbow instead of skimming up that shimmering fabric and cupping her firm, high breasts. His gaze dipped inevitably and he saw her nipples tighten as if responding to the hunger inside him.

'Oh!' She stamped her foot on his but she was barefoot and it had no impact. 'Let me go. Now!' She thrashed in his hold, trying to get free.

'Be still, Jacqueline. You'll—'

'Don't you *dare* "Jacqueline" me. It's Jacqui. Or Jack.' Her mouth trembled and pain smacked him in the chest.

'You've got it wrong.'

'Oh, I have, have I? So you didn't come stomping after me to tell me I shouldn't have worn this?'

'No. Yes.' Asim gritted his teeth, infuriated with himself as much as her. Even now he couldn't believe his behaviour. He'd insulted her, grabbed her, hurt her. *Spent the whole evening lusting after her.* 'You don't understand.' Hell, *he* didn't understand! Where was his calm? His easy charm? Where was his dislike of reporters?

Her eyebrows arched. 'It's late, Your Highness, and we've both said enough. If you'd refrain from manhandling me, I'll be on my way.'

'Manhandling you?' Frustration ignited, fanned into a roaring inferno by guilt and raw need. '*This* is manhandling.'

He grabbed her other arm and swung her round, pushing her backwards. He heard a soft 'Ooh,' of surprise as her back hit the wall. Those mysterious eyes opened wide as if for the first time she sensed what it was to be at a man's mercy.

Not that he'd harm her. He just wanted her to shut up and listen.

Her tongue darted out to slick her lower lip and heat drilled into his belly. It was a habit she had when nervous. The first few times she'd come to his office, only that had given away the fact she knew how precarious her position was, that he'd look for any excuse to get rid of her.

Now, as then, the unconscious movement tore at his self-control. That mouth of hers…

Consciously he relaxed his grip, but not enough for her to slip away. To be sure he stepped in close so they stood toe-to-toe, their breaths mingling.

'I shouldn't have spoken like that.' His words sounded stilted, emerging from stiff lips. He wasn't used to apologising. He wasn't used to letting emotions get out of hand or blurting words before he considered them. He was renowned for diplomacy!

'No, you shouldn't.' Her eyes narrowed like laser-sharp sunbeams, scoring his skin. 'But you've made your point and I want you to let me go. I'm very tired.'

Liar. The energy running through her slender frame all but gave off sparks. His hands tingled just holding her through the silken sleeves.

Asim slammed a door on his thoughts before he could contemplate holding her bare flesh.

'I didn't mean what you think.'

'Of course you didn't. I must have imagined it all.' Sarcasm dripped from each syllable, but it didn't quite mask her hurt, and again Asim felt pain stab him in the gut.

He'd known she was affected by recent trauma but how could he have guessed she also had a warped self-image? It seemed impossible that a woman so intelligent and feisty should so underestimate herself.

'You think you don't look glamorous and sexy?' He couldn't quite keep the disbelief from his voice.

She stood ramrod-stiff. 'Don't! You've said enough on the subject.'

Asim shook his head, his gaze locked on hers. That fiery stare sent blasts of heat running through his blood.

'I didn't say it right. My complaint wasn't that you looked...' He searched for a word then remembered her usual camouflaging clothes. 'Drab.' He heard her swift intake of breath. 'It was because you sashayed into the dining salon looking like sex in heels. You turned every male head and sent the ambient temperature soaring.'

'Why are you doing this?' Her voice was ragged, her mouth tight as she skewered him with wide, hurt eyes.

'Because you don't believe me.'

'Of course I don't believe you! It's nonsense. The place was littered with beautiful women. You were surrounded by them. What would it matter if I...?'

Her words petered out and abruptly she turned her head away. Instantly, like a switch flicking off, the current of electricity arcing between them died.

'If you distracted every man in the room?' Asim didn't want to think about that but it was too late. He already knew the answer.

Because he wanted her for himself.

He'd felt sick to his stomach when her companion had spent the evening leering at her. Asim knew every man there had imagined tearing that dress away and having her for themselves.

Inexplicably Asim had felt betrayed. *He'd* been the only one to know her secret—that beneath those unflattering clothes lurked a delicious body ripe for the plucking. Now the secret was out.

'Because,' he ground out, 'I didn't want every other man there wanting you too.'

Her face swung back, eyes locking with his, and the shock of urgent hunger slammed into him again.

She just had to look at him…

'I don't know what game you think you're playing but it's not funny.' Her voice was brittle. 'I've had enough.'

Asim told himself to release her, to talk to her again in the sterile safety of his office, not in the dim seclusion of the old palace where they were totally, tantalisingly alone.

The trouble was he hadn't had enough. He hadn't even started. He felt his control snap and didn't give a damn.

'Did you even look in the mirror before dinner?' Anger roughened his voice. Anger at her for tempting him beyond endurance. Anger at himself.

'Stop it.' Her voice wobbled and this time the jab to his chest was a knife carving right through his ribs.

He let go one of her wrists and lifted his hand to her cheek. It was pale as cream and soft against his knuckles. His hand drifted to the neat whorl of her ear, to the ornate, dangling earring that emphasised the bareness of her throat.

'With your hair up your throat looks so slender, so fragile. And these…' he flicked the silvery earring so it tinkled '…draw attention to the sexy curve just here.'

He bent and pressed his lips to the tender spot where shoulder and neck met. She started and her pulse jumped beneath his lips. The scent of her was rich in his nostrils and he licked the spot, drawing in her taste. Apricots, that was it. Sweet with a hint of tartness. And skin like pale cream.

Slowly he drew back, the air heavy in his lungs as he dragged in a breath.

'Please, Asim—'

He stopped her words with a finger to her lips and felt their lush promise. His belly tightened.

'And this.' His hand skimmed the folds of fabric that fell in a curve from her shoulders. 'It's there to draw attention to your breasts.'

'But I'm completely covered.' Her voice had that husky weight that never failed to please him. 'I couldn't be more covered up.'

Asim nodded. 'Exactly. Whoever designed this knew what they were doing. All that lusciousness covered but on display.'

His gaze dropped to her breasts, high and proud and temptingly close. 'Are you even wearing anything under there?'

She tugged in his hold as if to break free and he slammed her arm up against the wall, the weight of his own holding her in place. To be sure, he planted his free hand on the other side of her head, caging her.

'I couldn't wear a bra,' she murmured defensively, and his body hardened. 'There's a slit in the back of the bodice.'

'Ah, the slit.' He surveyed her face, watching colour rise. 'It's masterful. That tiny sliver of pale skin when you move or turn. You have no idea how tantalising it is, do you?' Even now he read uncertainty in her eyes. She looked dazed but she held her mouth tight as if fearing to believe him.

'Sometimes a glimpse of the forbidden is more arousing than a blatant display of flesh.'

Her eyes rounded.

'Even these…' deliberately he stroked his index finger down one tight sleeve from shoulder to wrist '…simply make a man want to see what they conceal.' He breathed deep, relishing her sweet scent.

Asim dropped his hand to the shimmering folds of her skirt. 'This too.' He couldn't resist laying his palm flat as he dragged his hand up her thigh. Silken material over warm flesh, the combination was pure seduction.

He felt her tremble. Somehow the movement transferred

to his hand and it grew unsteady as he moulded her hip and tugged her close. His fingers spread, shaping her taut buttock.

'Tell me you're wearing something under this,' he growled, then shook his head. 'No. Don't. I don't want to know.'

He was rigid with arousal. He pulled her close so her heat cushioned his erection and his eyes sank shut, her gasp loud in his ears.

'Believe me now?' Asim's lips twisted in self-mockery but it was beyond him to pull back. For weeks he'd imagined slipping off her concealing clothes and losing himself in her firm, lithe body. Especially when in her enthusiasm she forgot protocol and argued with him, her face vibrant, her whole body animated. That was when he was in danger of forgetting himself. Too often he'd wanted to capture that quicksilver energy and naiad's body for himself.

'You're hard. For me?'

Her free hand fluttered at his hip. She wanted to touch him? The thought sent control spiralling.

Opening his eyes, he fell into amber fire. 'There's no one else here, Jacqueline.' She didn't object to him using her name this time.

'Every time you move in that dress the light shimmers on each curve and hollow. Did you know that?' He slid his palm over the tight curve of her bottom then back up to the gentle swell of her hip. 'Every delectable feminine inch is on show.'

He reached the belt of silver links and insinuated his fingers beneath it. 'And, as for this, it makes your waist look tinier than ever.' Plus it subtly gave a man ideas that would probably shock the woman before him. About chaining her to his bed.

Desire dragged at his belly and he had to force himself into stillness.

'I don't know what to say.' Her voice shook as she blinked up at him. 'Really?'

How could she doubt with his erection pressing into her belly? He was on fire.

'I forbid you to wear that dress in public. It's too distracting.'

Her lips curved in the tiny, delighted smile. He drank in the sight. It was the first real smile he'd had from her, not a polite social expression but a gift from the heart.

'I'm sure you could manage.' She looked down, the fringe of her eyelashes screening her gaze.

'Oh, I'd manage.' He snatched in a laboured breath. 'I'd scoop you up and take you straight back to your room.'

'Like a naughty child?' She pouted and heat zeroed straight to his groin.

'Not at all like a child.' Asim gave up the struggle with the remnants of his conscience and let his hand slide up to cup her breast. 'Like the desirable woman you are.'

'Oh!' She leaned into his hand, filling it with her bounty.

'Exactly,' he whispered from his suddenly parched throat. He'd wanted to touch her all night and the reality didn't disappoint. She arched, pressing closer, and satisfaction welled. At least he wasn't the only one drowning in this tide of hunger.

She looked up at him through her lashes, the picture of provocation. 'Then what would you do?'

His laughter was a harsh bark of self-derision. He was the sensualist, and she the woman who had to be convinced of her sex appeal, yet he was the one teetering on the brink.

'I'd make love to you till your bones melted and you couldn't walk.' He breathed deep, rapidly losing himself in the image he'd created. 'Then I'd do it all again.' His desire for her was stronger than anything he remembered. Outstripping his need for any recent lover. Far beyond anything he'd felt for the bridal hopefuls paraded for him.

'I wish you would,' she murmured, lifting her head so he read answering desire in her bright eyes.

Instantly energy crackled through him and delay was impossible.

Seconds later she was high in his arms, held against his chest as he strode through the night. Her hands clasped his neck and even that innocent touch sent rivers of fire rushing through him.

'Where are we going?' Her throaty voice was eager, not shocked, and Asim smiled. Only minutes ago she'd doubted her sex appeal. Jacqueline Fletcher was anything but predictable.

He darted a look at her face. That wide-eyed stare made her look almost innocent. To a man used to seasoned lovers, it was refreshing.

'To a bed.'

Despite the rigid tension screaming through his aroused frame, he almost smiled at her expression: doubt, trepidation and excitement.

'So far?' Her brow knitted as she pouted.

Asim stumbled to a halt. She was going to kill him. He wanted to find a flat surface and get her under him. Failing that… His gaze traversed the carved pillars lining the corridor. No. Taking her hard and fast against a wall wouldn't come close to satisfying his hunger.

'Unless you're carrying protection concealed somewhere.' His gaze dipped to her breasts, wobbling delectably as he strode faster, proud nipples erect beneath the fragile fabric.

His breath was a harsh scrape of sound as he finally turned into the corridor to his private wing.

'I can walk. You don't have to carry me.'

And let her go? Not likely. He wasn't releasing her till they'd finished what they'd begun. Besides, he enjoyed the feel of her in his arms.

'There's no need.' Ah, there was the door, just ahead.

'I'm too heavy.'

'Hardly.' Asim shouldered the door open and let it swing shut behind them.

'But I'm so tall.'

He frowned at the discordant note in her words and paused mid-stride. Something was going on in that convoluted, surprising mind of hers that he didn't understand.

Heavy…

Tall…

'You're tall for a woman,' he said slowly, watching her expression freeze, 'But that's good.' Her brows twitched in surprise. 'It means we'll be well-matched in bed.' His erection throbbed in eager agreement. 'I've been fantasising about those long legs of yours. I want to feel them wrapped around my waist when I'm moving inside you.'

Her mouth popped open in an O of astonishment as if he'd shocked her to the core. Yet she hadn't been shocked when he'd described his need for her, only eager.

'As for heavy.' He shook his head as he crossed the foyer. 'You're a lightweight. Even now with a little flesh on your bones you don't weigh much.'

'You noticed I'd gained weight?'

Of course he'd noticed. He'd been fixated on her body since that first tantalising revelation.

'This isn't my room.' Her head swivelled.

'No, it's mine.' There was protection in the bedside table and it was beyond him to last out any longer. Already his hands shook, not from carrying her, but from the effort of not ravishing her on the way.

Gently he laid her on the bed, his heart pounding with anticipation. Her dress flared like liquid silver, draping and cupping her delicious body. Already part of his brain was analysing the best way to rid her of it, even as he took a moment to relish the seductive picture she made.

Without turning, he yanked open a drawer and fumbled for condoms, planting a handful on top of the bedside table. Those amazing eyes fixed on the movement and she swallowed.

Dredging up the last grains of self-restraint, he dropped his arms.

'I want you, Jacqueline.' So much his chest felt like it was bound by steel bands. 'Tell me now if you don't want this.' He prayed he had the strength to let her go.

She shook her head and he nearly died. Then she stretched out one slender arm and his pulse revved into life again. 'I want you too. You have no idea how much.'

No game playing, no flirting, just honest need. Her direct-ness was more arousing than any erotic foreplay.

'Oh, I think I do.' Asim snatched her hand and planted a kiss on her palm, then pressed it to his chest where his heart thundered.

In one swift movement he was on the bed, reaching around her for the dress's concealed zip. She stiffened.

What now? His patience was worn paper-thin from hold-ing himself in check. Was this after all some coy game? Yet a look at her face disabused him of that.

'Jacqueline?'

'You first.' Her eyes didn't meet his. Instead she fixed her gaze on his high collar as she fumbled to find how it opened. 'Please.'

No woman had ever asked him to strip for her. Usually it was him watching his latest lover with anticipation.

'Very well.' He stood, quickly shucking his shoes, his hands making short work of the fastenings on his jacket. Moments later it dropped to the floor and he hauled his collarless shirt up over his head, flinging it away. His eyes met hers and the current of sexual energy between them almost blew the back off his skull. Her gaze raked his torso as if he'd spread a ban-quet before her and she didn't know where to start.

He knew where he wanted her to start. He was hard as the stone quarried to build this palace. His hand dipped to his waistband, his temperature skyrocketing as her gaze followed the movement. Then he thought better of it. Once he was naked this would be over in minutes.

Instead he untucked the end of his silk turban. His hand moved deftly in the familiar task but the intensity of her stare invested it with a sensual significance that turned his blood heavy, making each pulse a ponderous thud that reverberated low and deep.

Eyes holding his, she wriggled off the bed and reached for the fabric in his hand. It arced as she tossed it, a ribbon of bright silk disappearing beyond the bed.

Still she didn't touch him, though her breath wafting across his collarbone was pure sensual torment. His hands clenched.

Grave eyes held his then she spun around, bending her head, giving him unfettered access. Her nape was dewy perfection, drawing his lips as he unfastened the couple of buttons at her neck then tugged the zip till the curve of her spine was revealed, a sinuous invitation. He heard the click of metal as she undid her belt and it dropped.

'Yes!' With one swift movement he wrenched her sleeves down from the wrists so the dress slid off her shoulders to slither with a delicate hiss to the floor.

Creamy perfection filled his vision. He followed the sweep of her back and grinned. No wonder there'd been no line to mar the perfection of her silhouette. His uncertain seductress only wore a thong of champagne lace. It accentuated the perfect ripeness of her derrière and the tantalising swell of her streamlined hips.

'You're so beautiful, Jacqueline.'

There was no holding back. One step brought him flush against her, his erection snug in the groove between her buttocks as he bent his knees. Asim kissed her nape, his hands unerringly finding the soft bounty of her small, high breasts.

His groan was drowned by her hiss of pleasure as he rolled her taut nipples between his fingertips and gently bit her shoulder. A judder rippled through her and she stiffened, her breath hoarse. Then her hands covered his, pressing him closer as she arched, her backside pushing against his arousal, obliterating anything like a plan for seduction.

Had he ever had a woman so responsive? He bent further, raking his tongue up her vertebrae, tasting apricots and cream and the hot tang that was Jacqueline.

She shifted against him and Asim feared he'd come before he'd had a chance to feel her flesh against him. This woman's power to seduce astonished him. Her hands on his were desperate, the swivel of her hips not a practised, sultry invitation

but a jerky thrust of unadulterated need and all the more provocative for it.

Slipping one hand from her grip, he arrowed it to the lace
between her thighs. He needed to be there *now*, to impale himself in that delicious softness, but he couldn't bear the time it
would take to shuck his trousers and strip her thong away. Instead his questing fingers slid straight to her sweet spot and instantly she bucked, making stars whirl as the friction between
them morphed from arousing to incendiary.

Her hand slid down his arm just as he pushed two fingers
inside her tight heat. Asim felt the quiver begin deep within
her and ripple out till it became a quake that made her shudder and rock against him.

CHAPTER EIGHT

WHEN THE WORLD stopped spinning, Jacqui was flat on her back looking up into jet-dark eyes. They glittered, fiery, as Asim raked her body with a scorching look.

Gasping for breath, her limbs liquid, Jacqui didn't have the strength to cover herself when he zeroed in on her breasts.

Heaven knew what magic had happened tonight to make a man like Asim want her but she was past caring. She intended to revel in every single second of it. No doubts. No regrets.

A callused palm brushed her nipple and she jolted as a current of fire raced straight to her womb. She frowned. How could that be, after the climax he'd given her?

His hand stroked back and she reached for him, fingers curling around those wide, straight shoulders, revelling in the silky, hot feel of taut skin over bone and muscle.

She tugged him close. 'I need you.' The aching emptiness inside cried out for Asim.

He shifted, propping himself over her, and she felt the hard, hot length of his body, unfamiliar and utterly breath-taking. She'd been so dazed she hadn't noticed him strip his trousers. Heavy muscle and the tickle of masculine hair created a friction that was unbearably wonderful.

'Please, Asim.' But he ignored her urgency. Slowly he lowered his head and licked her breast and she gasped, her legs flopping open to cradle him.

'So lovely,' he murmured as his gaze collided with hers. 'I

haven't been able to get them out of my mind since that first night. So pert and ripe.' He lowered his head again and tugged gently at her breast, sucking her nipple till Jacqui's head thrust back and her body bowed up into his.

'And so sensitive.' His deep voice was smug. Through slitted eyes she saw dark satisfaction on his taut features.

She swallowed hard, a knot in her throat as she realised she'd never felt so close to beautiful in her whole life as she did now.

He cupped one breast and her breath hissed in ecstasy. 'They're beautiful. Like ripe, fresh fruit. I love that you don't need to wear a bra.' He paused, his brows bunching. 'Except in front of other men. But when you're with me you can go braless.'

There it was again, that domineering tone of a man used to giving orders and getting exactly what he wanted. But Jacqui was too stunned to care.

Since puberty she'd been conscious of her lack of curves. She'd never had to fight men off, like some female colleagues, yet here was Asim...

He dipped his head to suckle her breast and fire zapped her. She arched almost off the bed at the feel of his mouth on her. Was it like this every time? She tunnelled her hands in his thick hair, holding him close, and felt something under her ribs melt.

When you're with me. He made it sound like they'd be together a lot.

He's being kind, whispered a familiar voice. The cutting voice of her stepmother and the girls at school. But how could she heed it as she watched Asim and felt the magic he wrought? The glory of it drowned everything else. Heat drenched her.

'Asim.' She didn't recognise that rusty voice. 'I want you.' She'd never wanted anything so much in her life.

She dragged his head up, making him growl low in his throat as he released her nipple. Their gazes clashed and the febrile shimmer in his might have scared her if she hadn't already left caution far behind. 'I need you.'

His fierce expression didn't ease and Jacqui feared he intended to keep teasing her.

On a surge of desperation she shoved his shoulders, pushing him onto his back, rolling with him till she straddled his hips. The strength beneath her reminded her that she only managed it because he let her, a quizzical gleam in his eyes.

'You like to be on top?' His voice rasped gravel across each sensitive spot. She gasped as her over-stimulated senses threatened to explode just at the sight and sound of him and the furnace of heat that was his erection, hard and amazing between her legs.

She gulped as need and trepidation vied for supremacy. She couldn't bear it if he pulled back now. 'I just can't wait.'

Jacqui reached down to find him already sheathed and her pulse raced even harder. He was heavy and thick in her unsteady hand. She fumbled and almost sobbed in desperation, hating her inexperience.

Asim brushed her fingers away. Seconds later firm hands cradled her hips, guiding her as he thrust up in a long, slow surge of power that halted when she gasped. Jacqui couldn't help it—the feeling of impossible fullness stole her breath.

'Jacqui?' Asim's voice was husky with disbelief. 'Is this your first time?'

She clutched his shoulders, panic rising. She'd come this far, further than she'd ever been with any man, and she wanted it all, with Asim. All these years wondering and now...

'Sorry to disappoint.' She snagged another breath, feeling the tension in her body begin to ease. 'It's just been a while.' If she told him she was a virgin he might stop and she couldn't bear that.

Still he scrutinised her, his brow pleating, and she sensed his doubt. She licked her dry lips, her whole body trembling, waiting for rejection.

After what seemed an eternity he pulled her gently down, filling her inch by slow inch. She had to fight not to let her eyes bulge at the amazing sensations.

He watched her face like a hawk. His jaw was set, his nostrils flared, but it was the look in Asim's eyes that made her heart clutch. He held her captive with those eyes and she never wanted to be free.

Tentatively she rocked her hips, feeling the friction and the heavy throb of pleasure. When she did it again strong hands clasped her, helping her find the elusive rhythm.

He urged her high as he withdrew and bucked up, reaching, she was sure, right to the core of her. Lightning shimmered across her vision. Once, twice and she started to shake. A third time and her legs liquefied.

A tumble of movement and she was on her back, pressed deep into the bed, her vision filled by Asim. His eyes holding hers, his lips drawn in a grimace of pained pleasure, he thrust one more time and the world shattered in colour and light and sensation, overwhelming her.

Shuddering at the delicious shockwaves, Jacqui clutched him close as he powered on and, with a roar of triumph, reached his own pulsating climax.

The awesome force of his orgasm deep within and the juddering intensity of his steaming hot body surrounding hers smashed open some unseen barrier. Jacqui felt tenderness and an unprecedented tug of protectiveness.

She cradled Asim tight with the last of her strength. With trembling fingers she stroked his thick hair while he shuddered in her arms, his breath hot in the valley between her neck and shoulder.

Later they lay entwined, her head on his shoulder, his arm draped around her waist, his other hand spread on her thigh, holding her to him.

'Jacqueline, are you sure you're all right?'

Jacqui smiled drowsily, a delicious shiver rippling through her at the way he said her name. He made it sound mysterious and feminine, and for the first time in her life somehow…right.

'All right? I've never been better in my life.' She threaded her fingers through his. 'Thank you, Asim.'

* * *

Jacqui hurried down the wide corridor, grateful for her flat shoes. If she'd tried to run in the heels she'd worn last night...

She put a brake on her thoughts. Last night was over.

Asim had made that clear when he'd discreetly left her to wake in his bed alone. And she'd been grateful. She had no experience of mornings after and she'd needed time to process everything.

Heat swirled in her belly. Last night had been extraordinary. Magical. She'd felt desired and desirable, sexy and treasured. She'd woken to a sense of well-being that eclipsed grief and doubt. She was grateful to Asim for that gift.

Her gift to him would be proving she had no unrealistic expectations. He needn't fear she'd read too much into kindness and passing attraction.

For him, that was. For her... Well, it hadn't passed. The night together had only made her eager for more, despite the slight ache between her legs. She stifled a smile, remembering in glorious detail her unaccustomed exercise.

Jacqui buttoned her jacket and strode faster. She was late. Her visit to the old harem baths had been fascinating and the female historian informative. But, when the woman had learnt Jacqui had never experienced a traditional Jazeeri bath and massage, she'd insisted that be righted immediately. She'd said Jacqui couldn't write about the process unless she experienced it.

So for the last several hours Jacqui had been bathed, exfoliated, rinsed, covered in herbal concoctions, massaged and scented till she glowed. Every pore felt alive and she was preternaturally aware even of the scrape of cloth over her tingling body.

Or was that the effects of a night of hot sex?

She'd discovered she was a woman with needs, and she'd never been as aware of herself as a sexual being before. She'd never felt so happy in her life.

The shade of Imran rose in her mind and she waited for guilt to slice into her. It was a sign of the change in her that instead it was Imran's grin she recalled, his laughter. The way he'd always urged her to take chances.

Jacqui shook her head. Whatever her needs, she had to sublimate them. A woman had her pride. Sighing over Asim wasn't an option. Yet her pulse tripped as she entered the royal offices.

'Sorry I'm late,' she said to Asim's secretary. 'I got caught up.' Her hand rose to the unfamiliar silky camisole peeping above the deep V of her jacket.

She might have been on time but, opening the wardrobe to grab her trusty suit, she discovered a skimpy camisole instead of her serviceable grey top on the next hanger. There'd been a note pinned to it, an apology from Lady Rania, saying an accident in the laundry had damaged her top beyond repair and offering this replacement. As if Jacqui's ancient cotton top and this fragile garment—spun, she suspected, from gilded spiders' webs—bore any similarity. Even the shade of it, between old gold and amber, was luscious. And disconcerting to a woman not used to wearing anything that drew attention to herself, like bold colours.

Yet what could she do but accept it and hurry to her appointment?

Now, though, as Asim's secretary entered the Sultan's office, Jacqui wondered if she'd done the right thing. Her fingers fluttered over the delicate fabric. Against her skin it felt like a whisper, not clothing. A whisper that teased like the memory of Asim's breath on her bare skin.

Horrified at the sultry heat unfurling within her, Jacqui turned towards the water cooler, stopping as Asim's secretary returned.

'His Highness will see you now.' He smiled and held the door open and Jacqui had no choice but to enter.

Her mouth turned as arid as the great Jazeeri desert when the door closed and she confronted Asim. He stood by the windows, the glare turning him into a formidably large silhouette, his face in shadow.

Jacqui's heart hammered a tattoo against her ribs and she sucked in a breath, grateful he was too far away for her to register the spicy scent of his skin. It had lingered in her nostrils all day, a tantalising reminder.

What to say?

She swallowed and tugged her jacket.

Casual. She needed to be casual and calm. As if last night hadn't blown her self-possession to smithereens then put her back together a different woman.

Jacqui opened her mouth.

'Take it off.' Had his voice been so deep last night? It burred through her, stirring the blood in her veins.

She blinked. 'Sorry?'

'The jacket. It's an offence to my eyes. Take it off.'

At that tone of command her hand jerked up automatically to the button of her jacket before she realised what she was doing.

'I beg your pardon?' She tried to inject her voice with hauteur, but what emerged was a breathless gasp. She'd been prepared for embarrassment and the need to assure Asim she wasn't some lovesick fool. She hadn't expected this.

'So you should. It's appalling.' He crossed his arms. 'Wear it near other men. Never with me.'

Jacqui sucked in air. Again that hint that they'd be alone again and, from the gravelly undercurrent in Asim's voice, intimate.

She shook her head. She was imagining things. 'No thank you.' Best to treat his words as an invitation to be comfortable during their meeting. 'I prefer to keep it on.'

'And I prefer never to see it again.' He paused and when he spoke again his voice was a sultry ribbon of invitation. 'Take it off for me, Jacqueline. Or should I come across and do it for you?'

His words terrified her. It was one thing to tell herself she could pretend to be aloof and quite another to do it if he came near.

She fumbled the button open then peeled the jacket off,

covering the wash of heat across her bare arms and shoulders by taking her time putting it on a chair.

When she turned back she heard a sharp intake of breath.

'Lovely,' he murmured in a voice that turned her blood to sweet, heavy syrup. 'As lovely as I recalled. And you remembered not to wear a bra for me.' His words scraped to the core of her where her insides seemed to be melting. 'I approve of the colour too. You should wear it more often.'

Jacqui licked her lips, about to tell him the camisole was a gift from his grandmother, when her brain slipped into gear. He thought she'd gone braless for him? That she'd wanted to please him in the hope that they'd...?

She gulped, shocked. Wasn't that exactly what she'd done? She'd told herself she was running so late and it wouldn't matter if she was braless as no one else would know. But *she'd* known and with every step, as her tight nipples grazed cobweb-soft silk, she'd thought of Asim.

'Now your hair. Take it down.'

'No! Anyone could come in.'

'No one disturbs the Sultan unless invited.' He spoke with such certainty it hit her anew that he was a man used to having every order obeyed. 'Now, take it down.' Dimly she registered surprise as excitement rather than anger rippled through her.

Part of her wanted to comply. The part that had come alive under his touch and the velvet caress of those dark eyes, not to mention that potently deep voice. But this was broad daylight. They were in his office. They couldn't...

The molten heat between her legs told her they could. That she wanted to.

'Last night I stripped when you asked me, Jacqui.'

Is that what he wanted? A striptease? Her heart hammered so heavily against her chest she wondered if she'd feel bruised later. A shot of adrenalin, heady as neat alcohol, pulsed into her blood.

Her? Strip for him? Horror merged with excitement to skate

down her backbone then burrow through her belly, transforming into butterflies the size of buzzards.

She hated baring her body.

Yet last night he'd made her believe he looked at her skinny frame and saw a different woman to the one she knew.

Fear sliced through her and embarrassment. That pulled her up short.

Did she really want to go back to being the woman she'd been before last night? The woman who hid herself in nondescript work clothes? Even if all she'd experienced with Asim was an illusion, it was an illusion she craved.

Did she dare? Anxiety cramped her stomach.

Her hands went to her ponytail. A few practised flicks and her hair fell in waves around her cheeks and shoulders.

'Now the trousers.' His voice was gruff. She couldn't read his face. Yet even after a single night she recognised the edge in his voice. No matter how he tried to hide it, Asim was as desperate as she. At least she hoped he was.

Praying he was right and no one would dare enter, she snapped open the button on her waistband, lowered the zip and wriggled till the fabric pooled at her feet. She felt shockingly vulnerable yet daring.

Her skin was so sensitised the air on her legs felt heavy. She breathed deep and told herself she wouldn't regret this. She wouldn't allow herself to.

'Now come here.'

Gingerly she stepped out of her trousers, leaving her shoes behind, and padded across the carpet. With each step tension coiled higher, till she stopped before him. Now she read his expression and was glad she hadn't been able to earlier. He looked so fierce that heat licked inside. His eyes glittered as she imagined those of his warlike ancestors might have when they'd spied a trade caravan loaded with riches entering their realm.

She shivered and rubbed her hands up her arms.

'You're cold?' Still he didn't touch her. She shook her head and he nodded, a tiny, knowing smile lifting the corner of his mouth. 'You won't be for long, Jacqueline. Sit on my desk.'

She followed his glance to the antique desk, bare except for a sleek computer and a single tray of papers.

Arousal shuddered through her as she pictured making love on that gleaming surface. It would be hard, fast and satisfying. She wanted him so badly she almost obeyed without a word of protest. She, who'd never been intimate with a man before last night!

'You're sure no one will come in?' Excitement and dread warred.

'Be assured, Jacqueline. We won't be disturbed. My secretary has left and locked the outer office on the way out.'

Her eyes widened. 'You told him to? But he'll know we're…' She shook her head as words failed her.

A small voice inside jeered that, standing almost naked, she'd left it late to have second thoughts.

'Fahid is utterly discreet. You have nothing to worry about.' Asim stepped closer and at once the vast study shrank. She felt crowded, excited and aroused, yet at the same time annoyed.

This was utterly unfamiliar territory. Last night had turned her inside out, made her question long-held certainties and put her trust in a man she barely knew. Even so it had felt right.

Now, abruptly, standing half-dressed while he calmly gave orders, unease spiked. If only Asim had come to her, embraced her, done something other than bark instructions. Tension crawled along her shoulders. Indignation rose. She might be desperate but she had some self-respect.

'Do you make a habit of seducing women on your desk?' The words shot out and she raised her chin, battling to hide churning distress.

She didn't expect declarations of undying devotion but she wasn't some convenience, available to satisfy a passing itch.

Nevertheless, she had to fight her needy body that swayed towards him as if seeking a caress from its master.

He strode forward till they almost touched. His brilliant

gaze raked her; the subtle scent of his skin filled her nostrils, weakening her knees. He radiated heat that hazed her skin.

'I have never seduced a woman here.' He paused and Jacqui was surprised to see him swallow. 'My desk has been used for nothing but paperwork.' His eyes narrowed to glittering darts that scraped her skin. His voice was steely. 'I spend my days and many of my nights here working, not dallying with women. As for Fahid guessing...' Asim's shoulders rose in a shrug. 'It seemed preferable to have privacy rather than run the risk of interruption.'

'Because you were so sure I'd give you what you want.' And he'd been right. Jacqui had bared herself to camisole and panties, desperate for his touch. Were her doubts just delaying tactics so she didn't have to acknowledge she was putty in his hands? Her stomach cramped.

'What we *both* want. Don't deny it, Jacqueline. I see the flush of arousal on your perfect skin. Your pulse races and your beautiful breasts are rising fast because your breathing is too shallow.'

He was right. Her body betrayed her. She wanted him.

Yet she needed more, proof this meant something to him too. That they were equals in this.

Doubt lingered. Why had Asim made love to her? Had he been motivated by pity and mere convenience? Last night she hadn't thought so but today he seemed so cold and uninvolved. It was hard to shake a lifetime of self-doubt.

'Then why haven't you touched me?' Despite her intentions it sounded like a plea.

He shook his head, his face grim. 'Once I touch you, Jacqueline, there'll be no holding back, no time for finesse. I've spent the whole day waiting for you, and I'm not a patient man.'

Startled, Jacqui gazed up at that strongly sculpted face and felt heat squiggle through her. Now she saw more than his piercing gaze. A pulse throbbed at his temple. His squared jaw was set and the tendons visible in his neck spoke of tension. Tension *she'd* put there? Heady relief and pleasure filled her.

His big hands flexed as if resisting the urge to reach for her. The movement drew attention to the bulge in his trousers she hadn't noticed earlier.

Remembering the heavy, delicious weight of him, the softness of satin over forged steel, her inner muscles contracted. His body fascinated her but last night, though they'd shared more intimacies than she'd ever experienced, he'd been the one exploring her body. She'd had no chance to satisfy her curiosity.

'Sit on the desk, Jacqueline.' His voice was harsh but she caught an edge of desperation. 'I promise you'll enjoy it.'

'No.'

'No?' Asim's head reared back, his eyes rounding. He'd been so sure of her. And not used to anyone denying him what he wanted. 'What do you mean, *no*?' It was a roar of outrage.

Jacqui licked dry lips as excitement and trepidation warred. She made herself meet his eyes.

We're equals, she told herself. He might be lord of all he surveys but she wasn't his subject. Besides, something had changed after last night—the way he'd confronted her hang-ups and shown her they meant nothing to him. Her body hummed with arousal and a woman's curiosity.

'No, I don't want you to take me on your desk. Not yet.' For now she said it aloud she was shocked at how appealing it sounded.

'Then what do you want?' His brow furrowed in a scowl.

For a moment longer she hesitated, but her body, primed by a day of physical pampering and now by proximity to Asim, had no doubts.

She dropped to her knees and heard his hiss of indrawn breath. Reaching out, she flicked open the button at the top of this trousers and tugged the zip.

'This,' she said, reaching for him.

CHAPTER NINE

SHE WAS KILLING HIM.

Hour by hour she drove him quietly insane.

Asim frowned as strode from the stables. His ride hadn't cleared his head. It was filled with Jacqueline. Her sighs as she snuggled up to him in bed; the look of exhilaration when he told her how beautiful she was.

The spark of devilment in her eyes when she occasionally convinced him to let her take the lead in sex. He tightened as heat flashed through him. Remembering her hands on him, her mouth—hot and sultry and a little clumsy—brought him to fever pitch all over again.

He'd wondered that first night if she was a virgin, but she'd been adamant and he'd let himself be persuaded. Now he was convinced he'd been right. Jacqueline was passionate and eager but definitely inexperienced.

Or she had been.

Asim's jaw clenched. At least that had relieved his earlier discomfort that he might be poaching on his cousin's territory. Imran really had been just a friend. But now there was guilt that he'd seduced a virgin. A decent man would have pulled back straight away, respecting her innocence. But with Jacqueline Asim feared he had no control.

She was a *houri*, an enchantress.

She was disrupting his well-ordered life.

Was he mad, having an affair with a journalist? Logic should say yes but instinctively he trusted her.

He grimaced and entered the palace, nodding to a guard.

Sleep he could do without. He preferred to spend the midnight hours exploring Jacqueline's insatiable appetite for passion. She interfered with his work too. Those daily briefings on her research became long interludes that left him smiling and sated yet still hungry for her.

Worse, she interrupted his thoughts. Yesterday during another round of trade negotiations he'd found himself recalling her pithy assessment of one foreign diplomat. On impulse he'd changed his carefully laid approach to test what she'd suggested was a weakness in the foreign position. And the hunch had paid off! She'd been correct.

He should thank her; she'd saved him time and effort. Yet that crossover from lover to advisor niggled.

Asim kept his women separate from his public life.

That would change a little when he had a wife, of course. His wife would be intelligent and experienced enough to deal with diplomats, royalty and all manner of VIPs. But in the meantime it disturbed him that he found himself thinking about Jacqueline so often.

That was another thing. She stymied his search for a bride. How could he devote himself to that important task when the passion between them flared so hot? Obviously it would dim with time, passion always did, but in the meantime he owed it to himself, and his country to choose an appropriate wife. Yet lately the few he'd seen hadn't come close to arousing interest.

One had been superficially suitable: engaging, intelligent and well-bred. But he'd felt no spark of attraction. How could he spend his life with a woman if he wasn't interested enough to bed her?

Another candidate he'd mentally dismissed as too short. Too short! Just because he relished the fact that when he kissed Jacqueline he didn't have to fold himself in half to reach her lips.

Plus the feel of her long, slim legs locked around his waist was currently one of his greatest pleasures.

Asim grunted in self-disgust. At thirty-five he needed to find a suitable wife and start a family, securing the throne for the future. He couldn't afford to fixate on a woman as his father had done with his mother. Their passion had been unhealthily intense, turning into a sick relationship that had damaged all the family.

Starting today, Asim would do what he should have been doing: focus on his search for the perfect queen.

'I'm so glad my grandmother finally brought you to visit.'

Jacqui watched her companion twirl her long sable hair. It was a nervous gesture Princess Samira had repeated several times since Jacqui had arrived.

The princess was a beauty. The harsh, extravagantly male cast of Asim's aristocratic features were, in his younger sister, softened. They had the same hooded eyes, though in his sister's case they were a rich sherry colour. Her mouth was lush, not thin, and her jaw, though determined, wasn't uncompromisingly hard.

Yet despite her beauty there were shadows under her eyes and she had a lustreless quality as if weighed down by unimaginable woes.

'I'm honoured you invited me.' And intrigued that Lady Rania had left them alone after half an hour.

Jacqui's chest squeezed in sympathy as the princess fumbled the traditional coffee pot she'd been tending, her hand unsteady. She looked tired and fragile but her minuscule frown as she concentrated on pouring the honeyed coffee into tiny cups reminded Jacqui of Asim.

But everything reminded her of Asim. He was in her thoughts constantly. She spent the night flush against his big, naked body, and even when she dreamed it was of him, not the horror that had haunted her for months.

'Thank you, Your Highness.' Jacqui accepted a steaming, fragrant cup.

'Please, call me Samira.' The other woman smiled and Jacqui caught her breath at the impact a little animation had on her face. More than beautiful, she was stunning. No wonder the press was avaricious for photos. That face would sell millions of magazines.

It took a moment to realise the other woman's smile had faded.

'I'd be honoured.' Jacqui was surprised at the unlooked for offer. 'Thank you, Samira. And I'm Jacqui.'

'Not Jacqueline, as my brother calls you?'

Jacqui froze, the cup halfway to her lips. 'He talks about me?' Intimate as they were, she hadn't expected him to discuss her with his sister.

A mischievous smile tugged Samira's mouth. 'More than I suspect he realises. But my grandmother and I don't tell him.' She lifted her cup to her lips. 'Now I've begun to know you a little, I understand why.'

Jacqui wondered what sort of back-handed compliment that was. Except the princess struck her as genuine and friendly. And they had something in common: Asim.

Why did everything come back to him?

It was because he'd taken over her world, turning it from dark grey to glowing brightness.

He'd made her happier than she'd dared hope.

And he made her feel special. So special it scared her, made her worry this couldn't be real. She'd never felt such closeness, even with her family. Was she imagining he cared for her because she wanted it to be true? Was she extra needy because of the stress she'd gone through?

'Tell me more about your project, Jacqui. I was too...unwell to attend the sessions with my grandmother and her friends. But I'd like to hear more.'

An hour later they were on their second coffees and the conversation had veered through traditional Jazeeri dresses to the silvery grey designer original Jacqui had worn at the formal dinner.

'You mean you designed it?' She leaned forward, admiring the portfolio Samira had produced. There were sketches, fabric swatches and photos of finished dresses. All were stunning, ultra-feminine in an unfussy, eye-catching style that instantly appealed.

'Grandmother wanted to give you a gift.' Samira smiled. 'She is so excited about your book and the sensitive way you're approaching it. She wasn't sure you had something suitable for Asim's formal dinner.'

'I don't. Didn't.' Jacqui shook her head. 'I still can't believe you designed that amazing dress. And these. They're gorgeous.'

Samira shrugged. 'It's a very trivial talent, nothing compared with the work you do—'

'Nonsense!' The word shot out and belatedly Jacqui wondered if she'd been too forthright when Samira stiffened.

Jacqui had enjoyed their conversation so much she'd almost forgotten her companion's royal status, and that they'd just met. It felt as if they'd known each other for ages. 'I'm sorry. I didn't mean to be rude.' Even now Samira didn't smile and the shadows were back in her eyes. Jacqui wondered if it was just her break-up with her actor boyfriend that had wounded her, or something deeper.

'What I meant was that we each have talents and should be grateful for them. I could never design anything as beautiful as this.' She gestured to a photo of a blonde model whose evening gown of midnight blue swirled around her like a dream.

'You're gifted in a way that brings beauty into the world. Much of my job dealt with an uglier reality. It was necessary, because people have to know the truth about the world around them, but they need beauty too.'

Perhaps that was why her book was giving her a new sense of optimism. Despite the negatives to harem life, there was great beauty and grace too, personified by the remarkable old women she'd been privileged to meet.

'You should be proud of your talent, Samira. These are amazing. But you've only designed for friends? Why aren't you doing this professionally?'

'A good question, but not one for today.' Asim's deep voice came from behind her and instantly her flesh prickled in awareness. She drew in a breath, willing her pulse not to racket so fast, afraid her response to him would be too obvious. Since they'd become lovers it grew harder to pretend in public.

'Asim!' Samira smiled. 'I didn't expect to see you again today. I thought you were working.'

Jacqui turned. Asim filled the doorway, resplendent in a turban and embroidered tunic of dark blue. His stern features gave nothing away but suddenly she recalled his furious accusation when she'd first arrived, that she'd come to ferret out a story about his sister.

Is that what he thought? His hooded eyes were impenetrable but the line of his shoulders was stiff.

'I was stood up for my meeting.'

'Stood up?' Samira frowned. 'Someone cancelled a meeting with *you*?'

His gaze switched to Jacqui. Her blood sizzled and the breath stuck in her throat.

Suddenly Samira laughed. It sounded breathless, as if she was out of practice. 'Your meeting was with Jacqui?'

Jacqui blinked and looked at her watch. Samira was right. Jacqui should have been in Asim's office ten minutes ago. She'd lost track of time.

'Who else would dare be late for an appointment with you?' Despite the teasing lilt in Samira's voice, Jacqui couldn't find an answering smile. Not when Asim's scrutiny skewered her where she sat.

An apology rose to her lips but she knew it wasn't her tardiness he took issue with. It was that she was with his sister after he'd forbidden such contact. She stared back. 'I'm sorry, Asim.' To her chagrin she stumbled over his name. 'I'll come now.'

Still he said nothing and Jacqui was appalled at how that wounded her. Did he trust her so little after what they'd shared?

'Or you could stay too,' Samira offered.

Asim prowled across and put a hand on his sister's shoulder. His expression softened. 'I'd like that. But Jacqueline and I need to discuss a few things. I'll return later.'

I, not we.

'Thank you for your hospitality, Samira.' Jacqui got up and pasted on what she hoped was a convincing smile. 'I enjoyed our time together.' Far from being a pampered princess with no thoughts outside her social calendar, Samira was someone Jacqui wanted to know better.

'I'll look forward to your next visit.'

Jacqui smiled but said nothing, guessing Asim would ban any such visit, if he didn't simply banish Jacqui from the palace. Her stomach dived. He wouldn't keep her here if he thought it compromised his sister's well-being.

Lovers they might be, but theirs was a physical relationship, despite the late-night chats they shared about everything under the sun. An hour ago she'd have said they'd begun to know each other, sharing their tastes in books and politics and their mutual love of chess. But, looking into his dark eyes, Jacqui saw no warmth. She felt hollow.

Repressing a shudder, she followed him.

Asim remained silent as they traversed the palace. Instead of going to his office, they went to his suite.

So he could oversee her packing? Jacqui's stomach twisted in mixed fury and hurt as she bit down instinctive protests. She would wait till they had privacy.

As soon as they entered his private wing she spun to face him. 'I suppose you're going to accuse me of engineering a meeting with Samira so I could sell a story to the gutter press.'

'Are you?' He leaned against the door jamb, crossing his arms. He looked smugly superior, and devastatingly sexy despite that harsh expression.

Pain smacked her in the chest as she realised how much his

trust had meant. For he *had* trusted her these last weeks. The guard shadowing her as she roved the palace had disappeared the night of the banquet and lately Asim had even discussed some of his work, describing at least in broad terms various projects and negotiations. She'd loved the sense that they shared more than sex, stupendous as that was.

'Of course I'm not. You know why I'm here.' When he didn't respond she stepped into his personal space, so close her breasts almost brushed his crossed arms.

'Except you don't believe me, do you? One of your palace spies came tattling that I was with Samira and you raced to save her from my evil clutches.'

Pain scored deep. She'd thought he believed in her.

'Palace spies?' His brows lifted, accelerating the fire in her blood.

'You know. The guards who used to watch me.'

Slowly he shook his head and for a moment she'd have sworn amusement flickered in his eyes. 'Actually, it was my grandmother who told me.'

'She did?' Jacqui took a step backwards, only to find she wasn't going anywhere. Asim's hands were firm on her elbows.

'Not so fast, my little firebrand.'

'Hardly little!' She didn't need his condescension.

His mouth curled at one corner in an almost-smile that did ridiculous things to her insides and made her despair of her own good sense. How could she be attracted to a man who patently didn't trust her?

'Compared with me, you are. Deliciously so.' He pulled her in, his arms wrapping round her. 'Tall enough to fit me but slender and fine-boned and, oh, so sexy.'

She shoved his chest but made no headway. He held her and her insides melted like chocolate in the Jazeeri sun. Her weakness appalled her.

'What a shame then that you don't believe a word I say.'

'Who said I don't, *habibti*?'

'But you…' Her words petered out as she watched that smile take hold and turn into a grin. 'You let me believe…'

'I merely preferred to have our discussion in private rather than where we might be overheard. I never said I didn't believe you.'

'Then why didn't you *say* something?' She shook her head, the wind taken out of her sails.

One large hand tugged her hair loose of its ponytail.

'Far better,' he murmured. 'I like your hair loose. You look like one of our Jazeeri lionesses with that spark in your amber eyes and your tawny hair rippling around your shoulders.' His voice dropped to a seductive caress. 'I love it when you argue, Jaqueline. You have such fire. Such passion. And I want it all.'

He pulled her closer and she was stunned to feel his arousal against her belly. Instantly the fierce roil of emotions within transformed to familiar hunger as instinctively she moulded herself to him. Asim threaded his fingers through her hair, pulling her face to his.

'Yes,' he murmured against her ear, 'Like that.'

'No!' She tried to insert space between them, levering herself back from his chest, even though the movement pushed her lower body against his and the friction there felt so good she almost groaned.

'Wait,' she gasped. 'You mean you deliberately picked a fight to watch me lose my temper?' Disbelief warred with something unbelievably close to delight.

'I did nothing, *habibti*, but say I wished to speak with you. You did the rest and I'm man enough to enjoy the fireworks.' His hand slipped down to her breast and she saw stars as he gently kneaded the sensitive mound.

'You, you arrogant, conniving—' Her head lolled as he nipped her earlobe and insinuated his hand beneath her shirt, tweaking her nipple. Fire arced, drawing her tight against his body.

'And you don't mind at all, do you, my sweet?' he murmured as he kissed his way down her throat and delight rippled through her. 'Because you're not intimidated and making up is so very, very satisfying.'

Jacqui opened her mouth but all that emerged was a feathery sigh as she succumbed to his expert touch.

With a tight smile Asim swung her round so her back was to the wall. Then he proceeded to show her exactly how satisfying making up could be.

CHAPTER TEN

ASIM LEANED INTO HER, chest heaving, trembling in the aftermath of a climax that had blown him apart. Stars faded behind his closed lids.

He nuzzled the tender skin at the base of her neck, inhaling the scent of summer-ripened apricots. She shuddered and clenched around him one last time and impossibly he felt a flicker of renewed response.

Virile he might be but Jacqueline Fletcher pushed him to limits he'd never thought possible.

Was that why he'd sought her out in Samira's rooms rather than whittle down the list of bridal candidates? He'd returned from his ride determined to give that task his full attention and instead he'd given in to temptation again. He hadn't been able to settle as the clock had passed the hour for their usual appointment.

It disturbed him, how his usual control deserted him around her.

'Asim?' He loved hearing her voice like this, low and breathy. 'You should put me down.'

For answer he widened his stance, wedging her tighter against the wall, her legs still around his waist. He didn't want to let her go. He wanted her right where she was.

How long would it take to convince her she wasn't too tall or her perfect breasts too small? That she was beautiful? It didn't matter. He enjoyed demonstrating how wrong she was.

Except one day he'd have to put her aside when he took a wife. The realisation exploded his sense of well-being.

Some internal organ he couldn't identify clenched hard in denial.

He distracted himself by kissing her bare shoulder. 'You have the most perfect skin,' he murmured. 'Like cream. How did you grow up in Australia and not get covered in freckles?'

'I have freckles!'

'A smattering on your nose and a couple on your hands, no more.'

'My mother insisted I cover up in the sun and I kept the habit of wearing long sleeves. It wasn't difficult. Summers in Tasmania are short.'

She wriggled and reluctantly Asim decided it was time to move. The condom needed disposal, then they should talk.

Minutes later, after a slow kiss that left Jacqueline satisfyingly silent and starry-eyed, Asim headed for the bathroom.

His jaw set as he saw his reflection in the mirror. The dishevelled clothes didn't bother him, but the unfamiliar expression in his eyes did. It was more than sexual satisfaction. More than smugness at having silenced the most argumentative, feisty woman he knew.

There was something disturbing about that look. He wished he knew what it was. Just as he wished he understood his feelings for Jacqueline.

They were lovers—simple.

Yet he'd never let any woman so close. Physical intimacy was one thing, but she'd inveigled her way into other parts of his life, his work, his thoughts, even his decision making.

He'd come after her to warn her about Samira. Not to warn her off—and that was another disturbing factor. With Jacqueline he'd slid too easily past distrust into acceptance that she was a woman of honour who wouldn't harm his sister.

Asim breathed sharply, bewildered by his faith in her. Such trust went against every instinct. Asim had spent a lifetime standing alone, forced to rely on no one but himself.

His little sister had needed protecting as a child in the hothouse atmosphere of his parents' unstable passion. They'd been so caught up in their roller-coaster relationship they'd used her as a pawn in their battles one day and neglected her the next. Samira still needed protection.

His grandmother... He trusted her and cared for her, but she hadn't been there when he was young and now it was his role to look after her.

Yet with Jacqueline, who wasn't even family, he found himself wanting to share parts of himself he never had before.

Asim shook his head. He was not becoming fixated on her. He was *not* repeating the mistakes of his father. He was in control.

Jacqui sat back in a chair beneath a courtyard tree and closed her eyes, drawing in a shaky breath. As if that could calm her racing pulse.

She and Asim had just had frantic, raunchy, scream-out-loud sex against a wall and all she could think of was doing it again.

This was getting out of hand. She'd never thought of herself as highly sexed. If anything she'd wondered at her lack of libido. Was she becoming a sex addict?

Or, worse, addicted to Asim?

He'd tricked her into anger just to watch her temper catch fire! He'd been unrepentant and smug and she hadn't been able to resist him. She hadn't much put up even token resistance when he'd stripped her clothes away and taken her hard and fast and, oh, so satisfyingly. If anything, the remnants of her fury had added extra sizzle to the scorching experience.

The warm breeze stirred her clothes, reminding her of his breath on her skin. She sighed.

'Pleasant thoughts?' A finger trailed down her cheek, her throat, to swirl around her peaked nipple and she sat up with a jerk, eyes snapping open. Eyes as dark as midnight met hers and longing throbbed through her. To touch him, but more, so much more.

Shock hit her. She told herself it was the aftermath of the best sex of her life.

Pity she didn't believe it.

Asim sank into a chair turned towards hers. He looked cool and collected, as if she'd imagined the last half hour. Jacqui felt again as if she played catch-up.

'I want to talk to you about Samira.'

Jacqui blinked. 'I'm not going to do a media piece about her.' Surely he knew that?

Asim raised his hand. 'I know you didn't come here to investigate her. I know it was my grandmother's idea to bring the two of you together.'

'But?'

'You need to know my sister is fragile at the moment.'

Slowly Jacqui nodded. 'I'd picked that up.' It wasn't just the rings under Samira's eyes but her mention of having been unwell and her patent lack of strength. 'Being hounded by the paparazzi on top of that very public break-up must have been incredibly stressful.'

Since Samira and her boyfriend had once been dubbed the world's most beautiful couple, the media had gone into frenzy at their spectacular bust-up. Lurid details of his affair and the disruption to the blockbuster film he'd been shooting only added fuel to the flames.

'The press won't leave her alone. They want the inside story on her heartbreak.' Asim spoke through gritted teeth and Jacqui reached to cover his hand. Instantly he turned his, meshing their fingers and holding tight.

Funny how that small gesture stopped Jacqui's breath.

He was a remarkable man, the Sultan of Jazeer. His modern country still adhered to many ancient traditions. She imagined a lot of men in his situation washing their hands of an unmarried sister whose love life was so public, or who even *had* a love life.

As if reading her mind, he spoke. 'She's an adult and she makes her own choices. Living overseas seemed to suit her.

She was so excited about her textile and design course. She excelled at it too.'

He paused, watching a pair of tiny birds flutter in the trees.

'Then she fell in love.' His voice rang hollow on the word. Clearly he despised the man Samira had fallen for. How could he not? 'To say it wasn't a good match is an understatement, but despite her gentleness my sister is stubborn.'

'Possibly it runs in the family.' His head swung around, eyebrows lifting, and Jacqui shrugged. 'Both you and your grandmother have decided views, even if your grandmother isn't quite so...'

'Domineering?'

She saw the gleam in Asim's eyes and smiled. 'There are times when that can be quite invigorating.' Jacqui's gaze slid towards the entry foyer where he'd just taken her so thoroughly.

He laughed and the sound shivered through her, a rare treat.

'But not all the time?' His expression sobered. 'Suffice to say she fancied herself in *love* with the louse.'

There it was again, that condemnation on the word 'love'.

'When he betrayed her it came out of the blue and her world crumbled.' Asim scowled, his expression rough hewn. His fingers tightened on hers, almost to the point of pain, and she sensed suppressed violence.

Samira's ex-lover was incredibly lucky Asim hadn't exacted revenge. It would be in character, unless Samira had pleaded with him for mercy. Even the few minutes she'd seen brother and sister together had revealed Asim's strong feelings for Samira. If she'd begged him to stay his hand he would have done it.

'What you don't know is that there's more to the story than a love affair gone wrong.'

Late sunlight sneaked through the branches and gilded Asim's jaw. It might have been cast in bronze for all the softness she could see. A pulse beat rapidly at his temple. Once more she was reminded of an ancient warrior, eager for combat.

He drew a slow breath and eased his grip. When he turned she saw heat in his eyes, but regret too.

'Samira is recuperating from more than the shock of his betrayal.' He paused and for the first time ever Jacqui sensed him hesitate. 'I can't betray her confidence by saying more, but I want you to know and be prepared. Samira isn't strong, either physically or emotionally. More perhaps than is obvious.'

Concern etched Asim's features. She respected him all the more for not sharing his sister's private affairs without permission.

Her mind whirled. What could have made such an appalling situation worse? But it was none of her business.

'You need to know, to take that into consideration as you get to know her.'

Startled, Jacqui stared up at him. 'You seem very sure that's going to happen.'

Amusement lightened his stern features. 'I know you, my little firebrand, and I know my sister. Now you've met, there's no chance of keeping you apart.' He pulled her hand onto his thigh and clamped his palm over it so she felt the flex and bunch of hot muscle through his trousers. 'It would be counterproductive trying to keep you apart.'

Jacqui tilted her head. 'Because it's not worth the argument?'

He shook his head. 'Because you're good for her. She's been in hiding too long. I heard you telling her she was talented and should pursue her work. You talked about her gift of creating beauty and she *listened*. I saw it in her face.' His voice roughened.

'You have no idea how hard it's been to break through to her. Or perhaps it's that you're an unbiased outsider, so your words count more. Whatever the reason, I want to thank you for what you did today.'

Warmth filled Jacqui. When he looked at her that way the world brightened.

'You brought a breath of fresh air with you. I saw it as soon as I walked in on you two. It's the first time in ages I've seen roses in her cheeks.'

'When she smiles your sister is breathtakingly lovely.'

Asim didn't smile in agreement. To Jacqui's surprise, his mouth tightened. 'It's a burden she's carried all her life. Just like our mother.'

'A burden?' To Jacqui it seemed a benefit.

'Beauty like that doesn't guarantee happiness. It attracts trouble. Stunning women become invested in their looks and how people view them. As they age it undermines their sense of themselves. They panic and become demanding, needing more attention, more proof of their beauty.' He shook his head. 'It would need to be a very secure and confident man to marry a gorgeous woman. Otherwise he'd spend his life fretting over whether she's unfaithful.'

Jacqui opened her mouth to ask how he knew so much about it. But of course he did. His mother had been one of the beauties of her age. Jacqui had seen the press photos. Plus she'd skimmed reports linking his mother to one eligible bachelor after another, stories hinting all wasn't well in the Jazeeri royal marriage.

'Hopefully one day your sister will fall in love with a man who values her for herself, not just the way she looks.'

Asim snorted. '*Love*?'

'You disagree?'

'I don't believe in it.' Jacqui felt him tense beneath her touch. 'At best it's a fool's dream, something the weak hang onto.'

Jacqui frowned, disturbed more than she could say by his dismissive attitude. 'Your grandmother doesn't strike me as weak or foolish yet she believes in love.'

'My grandparents lived in a different time.' He lifted his shoulders. 'Maybe love was possible then.' He shot her a dark stare. 'Why? Do you believe romantic love can solve all your woes?' His look was sharp, almost accusing. She felt it cut, despite the comfort of his hand on hers.

'I don't know. I hadn't thought about it.' She'd never

dreamed of Mr Right sweeping her off her feet. She'd never allowed herself to dream, except about achieving her next professional goal.

Suddenly it struck Jacqui how wonderful it would be to have more than her career to look back on when she was old. How wonderful to share your life with one special person.

'What is it?' He leaned close, as if he could read the lightning-bolt flash that momentarily blinded her.

What would it be like to share her life with Asim? The trembling shock of the idea couldn't douse effervescent delight. A lifetime spent getting to know Asim, discovering his secrets as he uncovered hers. A lifetime feeling more special, more alive, than she'd ever been before. The idea was so heady she felt dizzy.

'Jacqueline?'

She met his probing gaze and found herself wondering if his children would have the same dark eyes, like black velvet.

She tried to tug her hand free. Asim simply tightened his grip, leaning towards her. Panic filled her and she went on the attack.

'Just because your parents weren't in love doesn't mean it's not possible.'

'Oh, but they were. In love.' His lips twisted in a parody of a smile. 'At least that's what they called it. I thought it was a battle for supremacy, one playing off the other. They covered it all—sickly sweet romantic gestures and times when no one existed but the pair of them, not even their children. But more often it was jealousy, sulks, rages and ultimatums, then break-ups and reconciliations. They tried to use Samira and me in their one-upmanship but they lost interest in us as soon as they reconciled.'

'It sounds awful.' Surely that sort of volatile, chaotic childhood would leave its scars? He'd hinted it had affected Samira. How had it affected him? Jacqui wondered if this explained why Asim liked being in control and having his commands obeyed. He thrived on order and logic.

'And as a result you don't believe in love?' She needed, desperately, to understand him.

'Perhaps there are some lucky couples who've found it, but I suspect most of them put a good face on it. The best you can hope for is an amicable marriage with someone you respect.'

'That sounds very businesslike.' Perhaps at last she'd discovered a cultural chasm between them. Until now there'd been little, apart from Asim's tendency to expect instant obedience to his wishes, to reinforce the different worlds they came from. As she refused to be obsequious, and they usually negotiated an agreed position when she wanted something for her research, she'd pushed that to the back of her mind.

'Why not? Marriage is the most important venture in a person's life. It deserves careful consideration rather than some impetuous decision influenced by a hormonal rush.'

Jacqui smiled wistfully. 'I can't imagine you doing that.'

'I should hope not!'

She looked into his severely sculpted features and tried to imagine him doing anything as impulsive as falling in love. He was so contained.

Yet Asim could act on impulse. Like when he audaciously made love to her at unexpected times and places. Sometimes he shocked her, novice that she was to this game of passion. He also made occasional impulsive decisions, though he'd label them instinctive, when he pursued an unexpected tack in his diplomatic work. Those flashes of intuition added to his reputation for brilliance.

'How about you, Jacqueline?' His fingers stroked the back of her hand. 'Have you ever fancied yourself in love?'

'Never.'

'Really?'

He looked so intent she had to ask. 'Why so surprised?'

His gaze shuttered and he looked away. 'I thought females were susceptible to romantic fantasy.'

'Not this one. I suppose I spent too much time with boys to see them as anything to fantasise about.'

'Lots of brothers?'

'In a way.' She paused, hesitating. Asim knew her weaknesses, her dreams and fears. What would happen if she shared her past too? She was used to protecting her privacy. Would opening up make her even more vulnerable to him?

He sat, waiting as if he had all the time in the world. The comfort of his presence, his touch, in this beautiful, peaceful garden worked its magic and she felt her shoulders relax and drop.

'Half-brothers and step-brothers.'

'Your parents were busy.'

'You could say that.' She huffed out a breath of laughter. 'They split when I was ten. But there were no fights or shouting. Just…coolness. One day we were together and the next they were moving on to their new families.'

His fingers tightened. 'They already had new families?'

Jacqui nodded. 'My father was seeing a woman who already had three boys. The eldest was just a year younger than me. My mother moved away and by the time she remarried she was pregnant with the first of two sons.'

'So you stayed with your father?'

Even after all this time Jacqui felt that familiar stab of hurt at being unwanted. Not once in her life had she felt truly loved.

Was that why Asim's attention made her so happy?

Her mouth flattened. 'No. They decided it was best to share responsibility so I went back and forth between the households.'

Asim shifted, closing the distance between them. 'It doesn't sound like you were happy.'

She lifted her shoulders. 'The boys weren't bad, though sometimes they really enjoyed getting their babysitter into trouble.'

'You had a babysitter as well as your parents?'

'No. I was the babysitter. My mother…' Stupid to let it get to her after all this time. 'My mother was more interested in her new family. I was a bit of an embarrassment to her and my stepmother made it clear I was only accepted in her house if I made myself useful.'

'And your father?' Asim's voice was terse.

She shook her head at the sight of the militant spark in his eyes. 'My parents aren't bad people. They never maltreated me. They were just more focused on their new families.'

'Leaving you adrift.' There it was again, that trace of angry protectiveness. Like when he'd accused her of having a distorted body image. Secretly she adored arousing his protective instincts. Even for a capable, modern woman there was something thrilling about a take-charge man wanting to make things right for you.

'I wasn't adrift. I made my own way. I dreamed of becoming a journalist and learning independence early helped.' He didn't look convinced. 'Besides, given the number of men in current affairs reporting, knowing how the male mind works is a distinct advantage. All those years coping with testosterone-filled teens was great grounding.'

Asim gave a bark of laughter. 'That would explain why you've never been intimidated by me.'

Jacqui kept her mouth shut rather than correct him. There'd been times, especially in the beginning, when she'd felt completely out of her depth and more than a little daunted. That was before she'd realised that behind his tough exterior and ruthless decision-making lurked a man of compassion and surprising tenderness.

'We're well matched, Jacqueline. Both of us are pragmatists. Neither of us is foolish enough to fall for the fantasy of romantic love.'

She looked into those gleaming eyes, saw his satisfied smile and felt some of her bright, glowing pleasure grow dull and brittle.

CHAPTER ELEVEN

ASIM WALKED WITH his entourage through the throng, exchanging greetings. They'd assembled in the plain where festivities were traditionally held. Once, tribes had travelled days by horse or camel to get here. Tonight, on the tenth anniversary of his accession to the throne, most had driven and some had flown around the globe.

There was laughter and feasting after a day of entertainment: displays of horsemanship, archery and shooting as well as athletics, dancing and horse racing.

Satisfaction buzzed. Jazeer had prospered and developed in ways that made him proud. He wasn't solely responsible, but his government had achieved much, far more than under his father's unstable rule.

He neared the gateway to the royal enclosure, on high ground abutting the citadel. The crimson and gold Jazeeri royal banner flared and snapped in the breeze.

Movement beneath it caught his eye and he paused, his breath locking.

How did she do it?

He should be immune to Jacqueline Fletcher or at least accustomed to her presence. She spent every night in his bed and they shared more hours awake than he had shared with any previous lover. Yet still she made his heart hammer.

His gaze roved over the slim figure in amber. She was stunning, a beacon glowing in the early evening light. Her dress shimmered, the long skirt moulding her neat hips and giving a tantalising hint of gorgeous long legs.

Immediately desire throbbed, as if his body had been trained to respond to the mere sight of her. He registered vague disquiet. This fascination should be ebbing. Instead it had escalated.

He wanted to be with her, stripping off that dress that flowed over her slender curves like apricot syrup. This on the night when he should be rejoicing in his achievements and the accolades of his people!

She made him want to forget his duty. He wanted to lose himself in her. Or at least be with her, seeing her delight in the spectacle and listening to her refreshingly honest assessment of everything, from the pageantry to the behind-the-scenes lobbying by guests. He sensed danger in the way she distracted him, making him lose focus. It was his duty, his responsibility, to keep control and protect those, like Samira, who relied on him.

Asim made himself turn. It was a test of willpower that he stay away.

His grandmother and her cronies would take Jacqueline under their wing. He'd remain here, doing his duty till it was time for the fireworks.

As the light faded and he finally made his way back to the enclosure a ruffled press secretary raced over to report a breach of security. Amongst the invited media, a cameraman and reporter from a major magazine were on the premises. A magazine that had pursued Samira relentlessly. Its staff had been banned from all royal premises. Yet they were in the royal enclosure, large as life.

Asim marched up the hill, barking questions to his stumbling retainers.

How had they entered? He couldn't believe his efficient security team had slipped up so badly.

But there was a conundrum. For it appeared the pair had press passes that had been checked and double checked and proven genuine.

Only years of self-discipline prevented Asim taking the steps three at a time. The Sultan of Jazeer never publicly showed haste or fury. He topped the rise and his heart pumped an aggressive rhythm.

It was worse than he'd thought.

A sweeping look took in the cluster of photographers held back by security staff. Their lenses were trained on the platform overlooking the plain below. On it posed women dressed in flamboyant rainbow colours. Among them he saw Jacqueline in full-length amber looking luscious as toffee and, in a gown of deepest violet, Samira.

Asim halted, pulse hammering, barely able to believe his eyes. Samira hadn't planned to attend. When he'd tried to persuade her weeks ago she'd claimed she needed time before facing crowds again. What was she doing here?

A barrage of sound hit and the sky exploded in fireworks.

Asim was stalking forward, his jaw clamped, when a hand touched his arm. About to shake it off, he looked down into his grandmother's concerned face.

'Don't worry. I'll get rid of them.' He started forward but her hand tightened.

'No. That's exactly what you won't do.'

'Sorry?' He couldn't believe his ears. The old lady had supported his strategy to protect Samira.

'They're here now. If you cause a scene it will fuel the flames. Look—they're not talking to Samira, just taking photographs.'

Asim followed her gesture, confirming that, while Samira was in full view of the press, his staff kept them from questioning her. The women came together in a neatly choreographed move and posed for the cameras, a burst of multi-coloured light adding to the spectacle.

'It's deliberate,' he murmured, taking in the scene properly for the first time. The beautiful women, the glamorous dresses, the backdrop of ancient fortifications and stunning pyrotechnics. The scene would enthral millions of avid viewers.

'Of course,' his grandmother responded. 'Don't inflame the situation.'

Grimly Asim nodded, forcing himself to stand and watch those vultures snap photo after photo.

Yet he felt betrayed. Someone in his palace had arranged this press intrusion and put Samira at risk. A few weeks ago she'd barely had the energy to stir herself and here she was, posing like some catwalk model for the paparazzi.

When he got his hands on the person who planned this, they'd wish they'd never been born.

Jacqui wondered if the smile she'd pasted on looked convincing or was a grimace of stress. These days she didn't like crowds and being on show, a reluctant model for Samira's gorgeous creation, shredded her nerves. But Samira had insisted, latching onto this opportunity with a feverish determination that convinced Jacqui she had to do her bit to make it a success.

Even though it meant keeping it secret from Asim.

No doubt he'd get on his high horse when he discovered what they'd done, but when he saw how well it worked he'd accept it was a masterstroke.

Of course he would.

But no one had mentioned fireworks.

Each crack of sound plunged her back into that day of chaos, blood and death.

The acrid scent of gunpowder turned her stomach. The whole display was torture, testing her resolve to the limit, cracking it till she feared any minute she'd fling herself to the ground, curling in a foetal position as the world shattered around her.

Another explosion splintered the air and she flinched. The hairs on her nape and arms prickled and she fought to keep the contents of her stomach down as terror iced her blood.

'That one was close.'

Mouth dry, she nodded at the reporter, trying to feel grateful for the mundane observation.

'And it seems to have been the finale of the show. Now we can talk.'

'Of course.' She'd been unable to think or speak during the barrage. Now she frantically drew on her reserves of strength, hoping years of experience in front of the camera would come to her aid.

She wasn't used to being interviewed. She'd shunned even her network's request for an interview after the bombing. But surely she could do this for Samira. Jacqui gripped her hands tight together.

Tentatively she began, confidence building as she followed the script she and Samira had developed. The interviewer tried to probe about Samira's private life but it was easy enough to turn the conversation back to what they'd agreed: Samira's dresses and her design style; the celebration; the magnificent citadel as a backdrop for what promised to be a blossoming design career. He even asked about her presence here and Jacqui relaxed a little more, describing her research and the generosity of the royal family.

'So tell me, Jacqui. What's happening between the princess and her ex? Our readers are desperate for more. You're an insider now.' The reporter leaned close, his smile gloating as he returned to his favourite subject. 'Just a hint will do and we can develop the story further.'

Jacqui forced her features into a smile, though she gritted her teeth. She'd known he wouldn't want to accept her 'no comment', but he'd have to.

'I—'

'You have all you need for your story.' A deep voice sliced through the night air, making her jump. 'The interview is over.' Long fingers gripped her elbow, turning her inexorably to face the tall man looming out of the night. Dark eyes flashed.

'Your Royal Highness.' The reporter half-bowed but managed to thrust a microphone forward.

Asim ignored it, ignored him, towing Jacqui away past security staff and VIPs. They didn't hurry but moved purposefully, though Asim paused occasionally to exchange pleasantries with guests.

Only Jacqui, with his hand anchoring her like a manacle of iron, guessed the tension riding him. It vibrated, a palpable force that sent shivers of apprehension through her.

'Should you be seen holding my arm?' she hissed between clenched teeth as the photographers turned their lenses towards them. 'Surely it's not a good idea to—'

'Don't presume to give me advice on appropriate behaviour.' His whisper cut like a blade. His grip tightened almost to the point of pain and Jacqui sucked in a shocked gasp.

Instantly Asim's hold relaxed but the angle of his jaw spoke of trouble, of fury barely contained.

'I need to see Samira.' Jacqui turned her head. 'She did so well but she needs—'

If his voice had been dangerous before, it was lethal now. '*Never* presume to tell me what my sister needs.'

A glacial chill crackled down Jacqui's backbone.

He paused and drew in a mighty breath that lifted his impressive chest, reminding Jacqui of the latent power in his big form. A power he carefully leashed when they were together. She sensed he was on a knife-edge of control and anxiety feathered through her.

Asim wasn't a violent man. But she'd never seen him like this. Even his controlled pace spoke of barely contained ire.

They left the royal enclosure, passed the guards and entered the passageway that led into the palace then wound confusingly. Still he didn't speak and with each tap of her heels Jacqui's tension screwed to breaking point. She should say something, explain, but her tongue stuck to the roof of her mouth.

They emerged in a garden surrounded by a pillared arcade. No lights shone but the moonlight revealed the old harem courtyard. A breeze whispered through the leaves of a climbing vine, making a desolate sound.

There to the left was the chamber where she'd woken from her nightmare to discover Asim standing over her.

It seemed a lifetime ago.

Asim swung her to face him. In the silvery light he looked as grim and forbidding as an ancient idol awaiting a blood sacrifice.

Jacqui swallowed and met his eyes. She'd known this would be tough. Keeping tonight's plan a secret had weighed on her conscience, but Samira had been insistent she needed to do this her way, not Asim's. In the end Jacqui had banked on the fact Asim would be so happy seeing his sister emerge from seclusion that his anger would be short-lived.

How wrong she'd been.

'I was warned against you, you know.' The words were a sliver of sound on the night air, slashing through her neat justifications.

'Warned?' Jacqui frowned, thrown by the change of subject. Wasn't this all about Samira?

He didn't let her go, just stood toe-to-toe, staring down at her as if he wished he'd never laid eyes on her.

She felt bruised by that look, her heart thundering in distress.

'You don't think your presence in the palace or my bed is a complete secret, do you? From the first I've had advisors warning me against you. Not least my press secretary. He said you'd cause trouble.'

'Now hang on there.' She stiffened. Asim's press secretary had been part of Samira's problem. 'I haven't caused any—'

'Really?' His head reared back, lips curling disdainfully. 'I should have known better. So what's your excuse? Are you saying you didn't inveigle your way in here by playing on the sympathies and grief of an old lady?'

Jacqui's breath hissed in. 'No!'

'That you had no compunction using any tactic you could to get close to us? To me and my sister, particularly my sister?'

Abruptly he released her and stepped back, his expression sharp and accusing.

Something cracked open inside her and she knew pain would

follow as soon as the shock wore off. Jacqui had expected concern over their tactics but not *this*!

'Did you think my staff wouldn't discover it was you who persuaded Samira to approve the press passes for those vultures?' His face thrust forward into her space, his demeanour intimidating. 'You think no one heard you promising him an *exclusive* interview?' Asim shook his head and Jacqui could have sworn she read regret on his grim features, not simply anger.

He lifted one hand and swiped it down his face, as if rubbing away an unpleasant sight.

The sight of her?

Hurt warred with indignation as Jacqui stared, disbelieving, at her lover. The man she'd grown closer to than anyone else in her life. Something crumpled inside.

How could he speak to her like this after what they'd shared?

What, sneered a tiny voice, *sex? You think that makes you special to him? How many women do you think he's had? You're just a novelty.*

Correction: *were* just a novelty.

She gasped as pain sliced deep. Her chest heaved and her head spun from lack of oxygen.

'Samira and Rania *trusted* you.' Asim's voice had lost that pulse of terrible anger. Instead it sounded hollow, like the aching void that opened up inside Jacqui's chest. 'And I let them. I *encouraged* them.'

He shook his head. 'So tell me, Jacqueline, what's your excuse? Money? They'd pay a pretty sum for a scoop. Or was it a chance to get back into reporting? Have you had enough of your self-imposed exile from the media?'

Jacqui opened her mouth but no words emerged. It felt like something had broken inside. It took all her strength to stand there, facing him.

She firmed her lips. What was the point, explaining herself when he'd already judged her?

With anyone else she would have tried, but with Asim…

He of all people should know her well enough to give her the benefit of the doubt. She'd *trusted* him, reached out to him as she never had to anyone.

Piercing regret filled her and she knew that soon it would be replaced by anguish. Oh, she could give him the explanation he said he wanted, but should she have to? What was the point? She felt battered in places she couldn't even name. Places deep within.

Finally she shook her head.

'Nothing to say? You surprise me.'

Yet still he lingered, hovering like some great, dark cloud about to swoop down and engulf her. As if he actually *wanted* her to persuade him.

When she remained silent, her gaze fixed on a point over his shoulder, he finally moved.

'Later,' he warned in a low growl. Then he marched away into the night.

Asim returned to the celebrations, accepting compliments and congratulations. Yet he acted on autopilot, his mind on the woman he'd left in the harem.

He'd waited for her to convince him there was some error, that her blatant betrayal of trust was a mistake. He'd *wanted* her to persuade him.

Even with the evidence of his eyes and the reports of his staff he hadn't wanted to believe she'd betrayed them.

He'd wanted to believe in her.

A flash of light filled the air, a thunderous explosion that turned heads and made bystanders jump. Asim whipped his head around, relaxing when he realised it was one final sally from the pyrotechnics.

But with the realisation came something else. Something disquieting.

Only now with a cooler head did he recall a detail he hadn't registered before. When he'd approached Jacqueline and the reporter, he'd been intent on their words, on what secrets she might give away. Now memory conjured up her tight, defensive stance, the way she'd flinched at the fireworks.

She had a fear of sudden loud noises. She'd admitted it herself, and he'd seen it the day they'd turned a corner in one of the palace gardens and frightened some birds that had shot up into the air with a loud clap of wings. The sound had been like a muffled gunshot and Jacqueline had dived for cover, only his grip on her arm stopping her.

She still suffered from the trauma of that explosion. Hadn't he soothed her more than once when she'd cried out in her sleep, her skin hazed with heat and her limbs twitching in terror?

Would she have submitted herself to the trial of a fireworks display for a cash payoff from some magazine?

His ingrained distrust told him, yes, people did remarkable things for money.

Instinct told him the scenario was wrong. Jacqueline wouldn't corrupt herself like that. She appreciated beautiful things, but her idea of beauty was more likely to be a faded, romantic mural than riches. The usher who'd shown her the crown jewels had reported she'd been as fascinated by the intricately embroidered silks worked by the harem women as by the fortune in gems they'd worn.

Asim frowned. If she'd wanted to sell her story, why do it here?

His gaze moved to where his sister sat with her friends and grandmother. To a casual eye Samira looked bright and cheerful. But Asim had known her all her life. He'd seen her pull on that smiling mask too often. This evening taxed her to the limit.

Doubt shivered through him.

No. Not doubt. *Certainty.*

He recalled the times he'd seen Jacqueline and Samira, heads together, chattering like long-lost friends. The way Samira, with her usual impulsiveness, had opened her arms to this stranger. And Jacqueline's rare, glowing smile when the pair were together.

She'd done this for Samira.

She'd braved the crowd and the barrage for her new friend.

How often had she said Samira needed to stop running and face the world? And he, so used to protecting his kid sister, had known it was too soon.

Whatever the rights of the matter, he had his answer. Loyalty, not personal gain, had motivated her.

What else would have got Jacqueline up on the dais in front of cameramen, dressed in one of Samira's sexy creations? This was the woman who still couldn't quite believe in her own physical allure.

Asim scrubbed a hand over his face as the enormity of what he'd said to her sank in. Her glassy stare and the stark whiteness of her features in the moonlight as she'd refused to explain told their own story.

'Asim?' He turned.

A lifetime's practice at hiding emotion came to the rescue. 'Had enough, Samira? It's been a big night.'

'It has. But a success, don't you think?'

'A huge success. And it was an unexpected pleasure having you present. Thank you, little one. I'm proud of you. It took a lot to face everyone and you did it in style.'

If only he'd thought sooner about what the effort had cost Jacqueline.

Samira shrugged. 'It was time I stopped hiding. After all, I haven't done anything wrong.'

'On the contrary!' His sister had been a victim, first of her scumbag of a boyfriend and then of the paparazzi.

'That's what Jacqui said. She said I should hold my head up and look the world in the eye.'

'Did she?'

Samira nodded. 'That's what she does when things don't work out. She said sometimes pretending to be confident, even when you felt horrible inside, is enough to get you through the tough times.'

Asim's chest squeezed.

That was what Jacqueline had been doing, parading herself in that slithery silk dress in front of the media, surely her worst nightmare come to life. And then to do it under a cannonade of fireworks! What guts that had taken.

Had her proud defiance as she faced his blistering accusations been her pretending to be confident when she felt *horrible inside*?

'Asim? Are you all right?' Samira clutched his arm, her expression concerned.

'Of course.'

He almost laughed aloud that he could lie so smoothly. Far from being all right, he was ashamed of himself. How could he have got it so wrong?

CHAPTER TWELVE

JACQUI WAS SITTING by the campfire when she heard the four-wheel drive.

She hadn't tried sleeping. How could she when her mind churned over Asim's accusations? Instead she huddled into her jacket as if that could counteract the chill that spread from her bones rather than from the pre-dawn desert air.

She'd thought to get away somewhere isolated and quiet. Solitude had always helped when things were tough. But now all she felt was alone.

Had Asim taken that from her? The last of her resilience?

The idea scared her almost as much as the slashing pain that tore through her when he'd looked at her with distaste and accused her of treachery.

The hum of sound became a roar as a vehicle crested the dune, headlights flooding her campsite. She clambered to her feet, one hand up to protect her eyes, her movements as slow and stiff as an old woman's.

The headlights dipped as the vehicle rolled towards her and for the first time Jacqui felt a sliver of doubt about coming here alone. Isolation didn't guarantee safety. If Imran had been alive he'd have scolded her for taking such a chance, haring off in the middle of the night into one of Jazeer's national parks. What if she bogged the vehicle in sand or got lost? What if she found herself at the mercy of men who had no respect for a lone woman?

Jazeer was generally a safe country but there were always exceptions.

Jacqui spun around towards her four-wheel drive as the other vehicle pulled to a halt. The door opened and the hairs at her nape rose. She sprinted for her vehicle and had her door open, ready to leap into the driver's seat, when a voice stopped her.

'Jacqueline!' Not just any voice. *His* voice.

How could that be?

Why wasn't Asim partying? It was his night. Her too-vivid imagination had conjured images of him celebrating with one of the sophisticated beauties who'd hung on his every word.

Their liaison was over. There was nothing to stop him taking a new lover. An unseen blade sank between her ribs at the thought of Asim with another woman.

She'd give anything not to face him now.

Slowly she turned. He stood silhouetted by the lights. Broad-shouldered and bare-headed, legs planted wide and hands on hips. In what looked like jeans and a shirt, he was rangy and hard as a cowboy.

But he wasn't anything so simple. He was the hereditary Sultan of Jazeer. His word was law. People raced to anticipate his wishes. He was feted and revered. And what he wanted he always got.

Jacqui peered into the darkness but saw no other vehicles.

'Where are your henchmen, Asim?' Her voice was harsh. 'No security staff to take me into custody? No officials to deport me as an undesirable alien?'

He paced forward, his tall frame looming larger than ever. 'Are you all right?'

The question threw her off balance.

'Jacqueline?' A sharp undercurrent bit through his words.

'Oh, I'm just dandy,' she jeered, planting her hands on her hips. How dared he ask if she was all right? 'How kind of you to enquire.' She breathed deep, shocked at how the sight of him affected her. She was torn between wanting to escape into the desert and the desire to fling herself into his arms. 'Or did you come to accuse me of stealing a vehicle? Is there a manhunt for me?' After tonight nothing would surprise her.

'I came alone.'

The timbre of his voice made her shiver.

'How did you find me?' She'd got permission days ago to borrow a vehicle for a research trip to the Asada oasis, but when she'd arrived at the garage after midnight it was deserted. She'd simply flung her bag in, grabbed the keys and scrawled her name on the register.

'Satellite tracking on the four-wheel drive. Desert conditions make it a necessary safety precaution.'

'I see.' But she didn't. Why follow her into the wilderness?

Jacqui sagged against the vehicle, exhaustion stealing over her. She didn't want to face Asim. Not until she'd shored up her defences.

'Why don't you come back here?' He gestured to the place by the fire where she'd huddled.

Jacqui stiffened. 'For a cosy fireside chat?' She shook her head, hair flicking around her face, reminding her that the evening's sophisticated hairstyle had disintegrated into a haphazard mess. She hadn't taken time to tie her hair back, or even remove the make-up Samira had painted on her. 'You've already said everything.'

'Not everything, Jacqueline.' She wished she could see his expression rather than just his silhouette against the headlights.

She stood mute. Instinct told her to run, get as far from Asim as she could. She couldn't take more of this slashing pain. Logic told her he'd simply follow. He knew the desert and she had no hope of escaping.

Pride locked her knees. She refused to retreat again.

'Please?' He sounded as uncomfortable as she felt.

Finally, with a ragged shrug, she stepped forward. What choice did she have?

Stiffly she took her seat by the fire, aware of Asim standing to one side. She'd been right. Worn denim clung to his muscled thighs and he wore a black sweater and serviceable boots. She almost wished he wore his regal finery. He looked too potently masculine, too approachable and real in casual clothes.

Real enough to rip shreds off her, she reminded herself, wrapping her arms tight around herself.

Finally he sank cross-legged to the ground on the other side of the fire. The easy movement reminded her of the fluid strength in his hard-packed body. A strength that had always attracted, even awed, her.

Jacqui hunched her shoulders, dragging her gaze away.

'If you're not here to arrest or deport me, why *are* you here?'

'To apologise.'

The prompt response stunned her and she found herself staring across the embers into a face of forged bronze and shadows. Something quick and hungry sparked between them as Jacqui met Asim's eyes. She blinked, telling herself it was a trick of the light or her own stupid, yearning heart.

That same heart catalogued his taut features and she could almost pretend to find regret and shame there. Shame? Not likely. Not from a man like Asim.

'You don't say anything.'

Jacqui shook her head, not trusting her voice. Asim apologising? Was anything so unlikely? Even if he'd learned the truth, since when did an absolute monarch feel the need to apologise?

'You don't believe me?'

She swallowed, her throat arid as the desert around them. 'I don't pretend to understand you, Asim.' She'd thought she knew him, that he knew her too, but she'd deluded herself. To-night's outburst confirmed that.

Slowly he nodded, his eyes never leaving hers. 'It's not easy, what's between us.'

'There's nothing between us!' Not after what he'd said. He'd lacerated that fragile, delicate thing between them.

'If that were true I'd be in the palace, sleeping the sleep of the just.' His lips twisted. 'Or entertaining a new lover in my bed.'

Jacqui couldn't prevent her gasp as ice pierced her breast and ripped through her insides.

'Exactly.' His eyes bored into hers as if he delved deep into her secrets, to the woman she'd never shared with anyone. 'There's still this connection and even my suspicions and disappointment couldn't sever it.'

'You're wrong, Asim. You *have* severed it. I feel nothing for you. I don't even know why you're here.'

His stare unnerved her. It took all her willpower not to fidget, to pretend she felt whole instead of raw and bleeding.

'Do you have any idea how I felt when I went to your room and couldn't find you?'

'Relieved? Triumphant?'

Slowly he turned his head from side to side. 'Gutted. As if someone had taken a dagger to my belly.'

Jacqui stared, her mouth gaping. Had he really felt it too? That slash of pain? Asim was many things: autocratic, suspicious, tender, thoughtful, assertive and generous, but never vulnerable.

'You're lying,' she croaked. But as she said it she knew that was one thing she'd never accuse him of—dishonesty.

Yet to believe him meant he cared about her, which he'd already proved impossible. Jacqui frowned, her thoughts tumbling over themselves.

'Why would I lie?' He leaned closer. 'You think I *enjoy* admitting this?' He paused and Jacqui felt his hesitation like a weight.

'I couldn't find you in my suite, or yours. I couldn't find your clothes, except those two evening dresses, and I felt...' He shook his head, his mouth a grim, flat line.

'Do you understand the dangers you face out here?'

The abrupt change of subject disorientated Jacqui and she shook her head.

'The dunes are treacherous. What if you'd rolled the vehicle?' His eyes flashed. 'What if you'd hurt yourself with no one knowing where you are?'

'But I didn't.' Her brow puckered. He hadn't chased after her in case she ran into car trouble.

'And you're alone.'

'I'm an adult. I'm used to being alone.' Independence had been bred into her early. Conveniently she ignored the fact that usually when she'd travelled in risky locations she'd been with Imran or another colleague.

'A woman alone can be vulnerable to unscrupulous men.' He paused, letting that sink in. 'And you know about our lions?'

Jacqui stiffened, her eyes frantically scanning the darkness beyond the firelight. 'No one mentioned lions.'

'Jazeer was famous for them and there's a tradition that, while lions live in the Jazeeri wilderness, our people will remain safe from external threat. Over the years their numbers dwindled to near extinction but in the last decade there's been a programme to re-establish them in this national park.'

'Not here?' She shivered, remembering a pride of lions she'd seen in Africa devouring some poor antelope.

'In an enclosure not too far away. Rangers have stopped poachers trying to kill them for so-called sport.' He paused, his expression grim. 'It's dangerous for you here alone. Such men flout the law. I doubt they'd respect an unprotected woman.'

'You came here to make sure I was safe?' Jacqui's jaw tilted. She wasn't some chattel to be protected.

'Partly that.' He lifted one hand and raked it through his dark hair, leaving it rumpled. Jacqui remembered the feel of it through her fingers, like a soft, thick pelt inviting her touch. A twinge of heat flickered.

'I had to know you were safe. And we have to talk.'

'You've already said more than enough.' She didn't have the stomach for more. She wasn't sure how much longer she could stop her hurt showing. Pride only stretched so far. 'It's late, Asim. I'm tired and fed up. You've seen for yourself that I'm fine. Why don't you go back to your palace and leave me be?'

His arm dropped. 'Because I was wrong.'

'Pardon?' Jacqui felt her eyes bulge.

'I made a mistake.' His eyes locked on hers, sending a sizzle through her blood. 'I jumped to conclusions when I should have known better. I accused you of dishonesty, of manipulating my sister for your own ends, and I was wrong. Totally wrong.'

Silence engulfed them, but for the soft crackle of the low fire and a faint whisper across the sand. Jacqui held herself taut, disorientated and almost scared of what he might say next.

'I behaved badly, Jacqueline, and I ask your forgiveness. I realise you were doing what you thought best for Samira.'

Jacqui leaned back, as if to sever the force field that drew her towards him. It was harder than it should have been, re-sisting the temptation to believe him.

'How do you know? What did Samira tell you?' Sourness filled her mouth. How easy for him to believe her now his sister had revealed the truth. Yet when Jacqui had needed his trust it hadn't been forthcoming.

Asim shook his head. 'It wasn't Samira. I knew as soon as I returned to the celebrations and more fireworks exploded. Finally my brain kicked into gear. If you'd wanted to sell a scoop, you wouldn't have picked anywhere so public. If you'd betrayed us you'd have done it quietly, not surrounded by my people and loud detonations. The whole scenario was wrong.'

He leaned forward and Jacqui thought she saw tenderness in his eyes. 'I realised too late how strong you'd been, support-ing Samira when she most needed it. How much you gave of yourself to help her. I should have been thanking you, not at-tacking you. An apology isn't sufficient but, believe me, I'm sorry for what I said, what I believed.'

Jacqui read sincerity in his expression and heard the warmth in his voice, yet something held her back. He'd destroyed some-thing inside her with his mistrust. She wasn't ready to let him close again.

She'd never let anyone as close as Asim, not even Imran, and tonight's devastating events proved how dangerous that was. She'd opened herself to a world of hurt. She should have known better. Her family had taught her she didn't have what it took to inspire love but she'd thought at least Asim respected her. His rejection after slowly winning her trust and her regard had shattered her.

But, oh, it was tempting to accept his change of heart. Her weaker side wanted to forget his earlier contempt and pretend tonight hadn't happened.

'If only Samira had confided in me this wouldn't have happened.'

But it had, Jacqui thought miserably. Nothing could erase it.

Was she being precious, too wary to accept his apology? But nothing had prepared her for the devastation his distrust had wrought.

'Samira thought you wouldn't agree if you heard our plans. Your press office has been adamant she remain out of the public eye. She was sure you'd take their advice again.'

Asim frowned. 'That's only ever been for her protection. When she first came back she was in no state to face anyone.'

'But she's better now. She's stronger than you think.'

'You believe I'm over-protective?'

Jacqui shrugged, surprised at how easy it was to talk about Samira instead of what lay between them. 'Isn't that what older brothers do?' She'd been almost wistful, hearing Samira talk about how Asim tried to shelter her.

Jacqui had never known that sort of protectiveness. You learned resilience early when you were unwanted. 'And your media advisor was all for keeping Samira isolated.'

'Samira said you disagreed.'

Jacqui shrugged. 'He could have reassessed the situation when Samira felt better.'

'So you came up with tonight's scenario.'

'Samira and I did together. As I said, she's stronger than you think.'

He nodded. 'She is. Between you, you've turned the secret of her isolation on its head. The press think she's spent her time working on what will be a stunning formal fashion collection. They're slavering for more. That sort of interest could be a springboard to a successful career.'

Jacqui smiled, relieved that he could see the positives in what they'd done. 'She's talented enough to do it too.'

'I can't thank you enough, Jacqueline.' His voice dipped to a low note that never failed to do funny things to her insides. 'You've been a true friend to Samira and my grandmother. You've given them both something they needed at a very difficult time in their lives.'

His intensity made her skin prickle and she rubbed her hands up and down her arms.

'It was only—'

Asim raised his hand. 'It wasn't *only* anything. When you arrived here I expected trouble and instead you've done my family considerable service. A service that deserved far more than my distrust.' He drew a slow breath. 'If there's anything I can do to make amends, you must tell me. We owe you so much. *I* owe you.'

Words trembled on her tongue. Hungry, eager words that would reveal how much she wanted from him.

Jacqui firmed her lips rather than blurt them out. She hugged her knees. She'd experienced so much with Asim, more than she'd ever expected, and still she wanted more. The depth of her neediness scared her. Was there no end to it?

Better to keep her distance. After all, though he'd apologised, he'd made no move to close the gap between them. Wasn't it safer that way?

Yet she couldn't staunch the slow bleed of hope and happiness. She wanted to be held and caressed and treasured.

The realisation almost stopped the air in her lungs. She'd begun to want too much.

'There's nothing I need,' she said briskly. 'Except to finish my research.' Turning from his searching gaze, she looked towards the rising sun, a glimmer on the horizon. 'I plan to visit the Asada oasis before I leave Jazeer. It used to be a favourite with the royal harem ladies and I want to take photos.'

The idea of leaving was like a physical blow. Her time in the palace had passed too quickly. She'd lived from day to day, not daring to think ahead, throwing herself into her project and immersing herself in the wonder that was her affair with Asim. Each day had been a revelation to a woman who'd thought never to smile again.

But her time was up. Regret shivered down her backbone.

Even if Asim's distrust hadn't shattered her illusory peace, the realisation of her vulnerability to him would have.

'We can do better than that. I'll take you to the oasis and you can stay in the royal pavilion there. It's rarely used, but I guarantee you'll love the old rooms.' His tender smile made Jacqui's stomach dip. She almost cried out at the sense of loss engulfing her.

It was one thing to know their affair was over. It was another to find the courage to move on. She couldn't seem to switch off her feelings.

'Thank you, but I couldn't impose.'

'Don't treat me like a stranger, Jacqueline.' His smile died, his voice turning harsh.

Why she fidgeted under his gaze, she didn't know. He was the one who'd been at fault, not her.

But he was trying to make amends, wasn't he?

The trouble was she wanted more than access to royal buildings from Asim. Much more.

She wanted his arms around her in the night when she woke from a nightmare. She wanted that gleam in his eyes as they made small talk at some official reception, promising delicious intimacies to come. She even wanted to debate politics with him! Spending a tranquil hour chatting with Asim at the end of the day had become one of her greatest pleasures.

Now she felt bereft.

It struck her how rootless she was. For years she'd had no real home. Visits to family were short and infrequent and her flat was a spartan place she didn't miss. She'd felt more at home in Asim's palace than she could remember feeling any time in the last eighteen years.

What did that say about her life?

Asim tossed a piece of wood onto the fire, watched the sparks flash and heard the greedy hiss as flames took hold. In the flare of light Jacqueline's face was pensive, almost sad.

His gut twisted. He needed her smile, her gurgle of throaty laughter, the flash of animation in her sultry, amber eyes.

He needed *her*.

The realisation was stark and undeniable.

He needed her as he'd needed no other woman.

That made a mockery of his attempts to negotiate a compromise.

He didn't want compromise! He wanted Jacqueline.

It was only now he'd lost her that he understood how important she was.

Asim frowned. He couldn't recall another lover having had such an impact. He chose his women for their beauty and good humour, for intelligence and sophistication. For their ability to please.

Jacqueline Fletcher was just a little too sharp and questioning, a little too unpolished. Yet she charmed his family, his courtiers and guests, and she charmed him. Her passion was instinctive rather than subtle, honest rather than practised. He liked her mind, her inquisitiveness, even her damned independence.

Even after tonight's fiasco the link between them was strong. The sizzle of passion hadn't faded, though inevitably it must. He'd known enough women to understand that. Besides, nothing that burnt so bright could last indefinitely.

Yet Asim acknowledged with a flash of disturbing insight that he'd never be content to part from Jacqueline till this ardour faded.

He didn't want other women. He'd even let his bridal search stall, distracted by her.

Giving her up wasn't an option. Not yet.

He had to win back her trust.

Asim drew in a slow breath and faced the unpalatable fact he'd been avoiding. Jacqueline wouldn't be won over by platitudes and a trite apology. She needed to know the whole truth.

She deserved to know it.

CHAPTER THIRTEEN

'You believe me to be overprotective.'

Beyond the flames Asim saw Jacqueline shrug but she said nothing.

He unknotted his hands and flexed his fingers. When that reporter had pumped Jacqueline about Samira, Asim had come within an inch of decking him. Hot fury surged and the need for violence had twanged every taut sinew. As if the man he'd spent a lifetime moulding himself into—honourable, thoughtful and judicious—was a sham.

As if he'd reverted to the unbridled, unthinking emotion that had been his parents' hallmark.

His sudden lust for blood, his desire to wrap his fingers around the reporter's throat, had made a mockery of everything he'd striven to be. Distaste filled his mouth.

'You know my parents had a troubled marriage.'

Jacqueline lifted her head as if startled at the direction of the conversation. Slowly she nodded.

'My earliest memory is the sound of fighting. Not physically,' he added quickly when he read her expression, 'Though there were lots of breakages. Ornaments and mirrors didn't last long in the royal apartments.'

Asim paused, remembering. 'I used to lie in bed, listening to the rhythm of the arguments. I became expert at reading the progress of a fight. I'd tell myself it would be over soon, when my parents kissed and made up, or temporarily separated.'

He shook his head. Amazing how some memories stayed fresh. His parents had soured his view of marriage and taught him that so-called love was a curse to be avoided at all costs. Was it any wonder he'd been in no hurry to find a bride? Shackling himself to a life partner, even in a carefully arranged transaction devoid of romance, was a step he'd put off for years.

'I protected Samira as much as I could.'

'They hurt her?' Horror edged Jacqueline's voice.

'Not intentionally. But she suffered. One minute she was petted and fussed over, and the next they were too busy screaming at each other to notice her. The poor kid never knew what to expect from day to day.'

'Nor did you.'

He blinked. Was Jacqueline taking his part?

'I was older. I'd learned to cope. But for a long time Samira thought she was to blame for their unhappiness, or when one of them stalked out and wasn't seen for weeks. She had nightmares for years, night terrors, they called them. I used to sit with her and try to keep her safe.'

'Surely you had a nanny or someone to look after you?'

Asim smiled humourlessly. 'We had plenty, but they never lasted. Either my mother sacked them because she believed they were seducing our father, or he sacked them because he believed they were spying for her.'

Asim rolled his shoulders.

'The details don't matter. I just wanted you to understand that Samira has always been vulnerable. She was caught in the middle of our parents' wrangling and she was distressed by it.

'They were never happy for long and when they were apart they spent their energy trying to best the other. Eventually my mother decided to use Samira to help her cause.' Asim breathed deep, ploughing his hand through his hair. He hated thinking of his parents.

'I found her being quizzed by a "friend" of our mother. The woman was a journalist and she put words into Samira's mouth, twisting innocent statements into appalling accusations about our father. Samira was thirteen and distraught, trying to set the record straight and horrified at the way everything she said was distorted.'

'That's awful! No wonder you don't like reporters.'

Asim permitted himself a tiny smile. 'Some more than others. I've learnt they're not all tarred with the same brush.'

Jacqueline's eyes met his and heat punched low in his belly. 'What happened?'

'Our father stopped the story, but years later rumours circulated. It was too late to worry about them. Our parents died suddenly in an accident and I had more urgent things to worry about than sourcing lies in gossip columns.' Accession to the sultanate at twenty-five, in a country damaged by his father's ineffectual rule, had been no picnic.

'The point is Samira blamed herself.'

'She was just a child! No decent journalist—'

Asim lifted his hand. 'I know. But ever since then she's had a horror of dealing with the press.'

'That was why she was adamant about me being interviewed tonight instead of her.' Jacqueline nodded slowly. 'She said she usually managed with a smile and a "no comment".'

'That worked until Jackson Brent.' Asim watched his hands clench into fists. This time he felt no remorse at the tide of loathing that filled him. If he didn't know it would make things worse for his little sister, he'd enjoy taking the actor apart with his bare hands.

'A smile and no comment is probably the best thing she could have done,' Jacqueline said. 'It lifted her above the rest of the players in that little drama. It showed she has class and integrity. She won a lot of sympathy.'

'She shouldn't have to win public sympathy!' The words slid out between gritted teeth.

'I know, Asim. I understand.'

He met Jacqueline's eyes over the fire and there it was again, that arc of energy, that link between them, as real as if she'd touched him. He read her regret and somehow it calmed him.

'What you don't know is the full story. I spoke to Samira before I came here and she agreed to me telling you.' He'd hated even asking.

'I know enough.' Jacqueline frowned. 'Her boyfriend, her lover...' she paused on the word and Asim wondered what she was thinking '...had an affair with his married co-star. Her husband caught them and is dragging his wife through an acrimonious divorce. Now the press are dragging up every detail of both their marriage and the relationship between Samira and Jackson Brent.' She spread her hands. 'Since Samira is gorgeous and talented, plus she's a princess with wealth and an exotic background, it's not surprising the press want her story.'

Asim inhaled slowly, a familiar weight crushing his chest. 'But what they don't know, what they must never know, is that Samira was pregnant at the time.'

'Oh, Asim!' Jacqueline's eyes bulged, her face a mask of horror. 'She didn't...?'

He nodded, his gut clenching as he remembered his sister, parchment-white and dazed, her face marred by the salt tracks of tears, lying beneath a starched sheet, a nurse hovering. 'She miscarried just after she arrived here. Whether from the stress or whether it was going to happen anyway, no one could say.'

Asim had never felt so helpless, so utterly useless, in his whole life.

'I'd always done my best to look out for her. It went against every instinct to do nothing when she hooked up with Brent. But I told myself she had to grow up some time. She had to make her way in the world.' He dropped his head, torn between shame that he hadn't done better by Samira and frustration that she'd made him promise not to exact revenge on Brent.

'I wasn't much of a protector. All I could do was look after her till she recuperated and give her privacy.' The feeling that the world had spun out of his control, that there was nothing he could do for someone he cared for, wasn't one he ever wanted to experience again.

'You did the best you could. You did all anyone could.'

Supple fingers closed around his fist and a jolt of power sizzled through him. Jacqueline had moved to sit beside him, he realised. Her arm was across his, her slim frame warming his side.

Asim clamped his other hand over hers, unwilling to let her slip away again. He didn't try to understand how her touch, her sympathy, could ease his turmoil. He simply accepted that they did.

He breathed deep, drawing in the scents of sand and warm, sweet woman, and felt that terrible roiling in his stomach quieten down.

'You were right, Asim. You had to let her go. She's not a child.'

He stared at their joined hands. They looked so *right*.

'Samira was so fragile, so distraught, we feared she might have a complete breakdown. The one thing I knew was she had to be kept safe from the press.'

'And then I turned up, bearding the dragon in his den. No wonder you hated the idea of me staying in the palace.' She squeezed his hand and, despite everything, Asim's mouth turned up at the corners.

'I've been called many things but never a dragon.'

'Really?' He caught a lighter note in her voice. 'But it's so apt. You're very fierce and proud, and handsome, in a dangerous sort of way.'

Asim huffed humourlessly. 'Don't forget fire-breathing.' His hold on her tightened. 'Jacqueline, I'm ashamed of how I reacted tonight. I saw you with that reporter and I lost it. I should have known better.'

Jacqui felt the ripple of tension through Asim's broad shoulder and arm. Regret laced his voice as he squeezed her hand and she felt the last of her fury fade.

She'd been hurt, unbelievably hurt, but now she understood what had driven Asim and why he'd overreacted.

'I'm not surprised you lost it,' she murmured eventually. 'Tonight pressed every one of your hot buttons: your fears for

Samira, your need to protect her, your distrust of the press. Even down to the idea of a female journalist taking advantage of her.' It all made a skewed sort of logic.

'But you didn't deserve that tirade. You put yourself out for my sister.'

Jacqui shrugged. 'She's a good friend.' Amazingly, after just weeks, it was the truth. They had clicked in a way Jacqui never had with another woman. In the past she'd kept to herself, focusing on work, the part of her life where she felt competent, where she *fitted*. Her friendships had been limited to colleagues and her job meant she was often moving on. Only Imran had been a constant, keeping in touch even when they weren't working together.

'So I understand now.' He paused. When he spoke again his voice was gruff. 'What you did for her—not just managing the press, but posing with her model friends to show off her designs for the cameras—that took real guts.'

Asim was right. Being photographed with a bevy of beauties had tested her. It was one thing to bask in Asim's assurances, quite another to parade for the press. Only knowing how much it meant to her friend had kept her there. Samira's need was greater than hers.

'Then there were the fireworks.' Asim shifted and she looked up to see his eyes fixed on her. 'How did you manage? You hate loud noises.'

Jacqui lifted her shoulders, arrested by the gleam of warmth in that look. Heat trickled through her where just a short time ago there'd been an arctic chill.

'I don't know. The first bang nearly had me on the ground, till I realised everyone was looking up and smiling. After that it was easier.' No point admitting every eruption of sound had jarred through her like the crack of doom.

'You're a remarkable woman, Jacqueline Fletcher.'

Her eyebrows rose. 'All I did was help Samira choose how to face the public. She just needed a positive angle.'

Asim shook his head. 'Don't downplay it. I know your

demons.' His thumb stroked her wrist. 'I've seen the night-mares and I've watched you break into a cold sweat at a sudden loud noise.'

Jacqui squirmed, trying to move away, but he wouldn't release his grip.

'I'm fine.'

'But you never talk about it.'

Her breath snatched in as tension clamped her ribs. 'There's nothing to talk about.'

Asim said nothing. Reluctantly she looked up to find him regarding her through narrowed eyes.

'What? You think everything would suddenly be better if I relived it all?' Sharp anger rose. He knew nothing about it! She'd been through it all multiple times in counselling.

'It seems to me you're reliving it anyway. How often do you dream of Imran?'

Like air rushing from a punctured balloon, Jacqui's ire bled away. No matter how she tried to escape, the memories crowded back. Memories of that day, the doom-laden sense of guilt and regret, rather than recollections of her friend alive and happy.

She shook her head, hunching her shoulder.

'Jacqueline!'

'What?' She met his stare, striving for defiance and finding only pain. She pulled air into her tight lungs. He refused to back down.

'Have you seen a dead body, Asim?'

He nodded.

'Have you ever seen someone blown apart by a bomb?' She snatched another breath, the movement jagging pain through her chest. 'What about a street full of debris, where it's hard to make out what used to be people? Living, breathing people who just seconds before were—' Her next breath was a sob and she stopped, sinking her teeth into her lip, trying to fight the trembling that radiated from somewhere deep inside.

'I've seen that too,' he said quietly. 'It's unspeakable.'

Jacqui's gaze lifted to his and held. She saw old pain and anger, and something that made her feel suddenly not so alone.

'But you weren't responsible,' she murmured. Asim was a protector, a statesman, a man who worked for peace in his region.

'Nor were you.'

Jacqui's eyes blurred. 'I led him into it. It was my fault. I had the scoop. I should have checked it out before dragging him in.'

'Why? So it could have been you lying there in a bomb crater and not Imran? How would that be better?'

Jacqui yanked at his hold but Asim's grip was implacable.

'Imran has people who grieve for him. Your grandmother, you. People who—'

'And you think no one would miss you?'

She lifted her shoulders, trying to imagine the reaction of her parents and half-siblings if she'd died. They'd have been shocked but would they really have missed her?

'You're wrong, *habibti*.' A strong hand cupped her face, lifting it till she stared into stormy eyes. '*We'd* miss you—Samira and my grandmother and me. And so would your family.'

Ridiculously Jacqui felt her lower lip tremble. She didn't cry except in her sleep when the nightmares devoured her. Yet Asim's tenderness unplugged the dam of grief she'd held at bay so long.

'He had all his life ahead of him,' she mumbled. 'And it was snuffed out because of me. I should have taken precautions—'

'Listen to me.' Asim leaned closer, his breath warm on her face. 'It wouldn't matter what precautions you'd taken. Imran was his own man. He'd have been there with you if there was a chance of a scoop. He lived for his job.'

His thumb grazed her bottom lip and she swallowed at the tenderness of the gesture.

'You think I don't know that? He was my friend.'

'But you didn't know him intimately.'

Jacqui peered up at Asim, trying to read his expression. 'If you're asking whether we were lovers, the answer is no.'

He shook his head. 'I wondered that when you first arrived, but as soon as we made love I realised that wasn't the case. You were a virgin, weren't you?'

Jacqui frowned. 'Did it matter?' She'd lied so he wouldn't stop. Because she'd wanted more than anything to be one with him. Her mouth flattened. If only sex was all she wanted from Asim. If only life were so simple.

'It mattered that you shared something precious with me, Jacqueline. Something to be treasured.'

The gleam in his eyes unnerved her.

'You were talking about your cousin,' she said briskly.

For long seconds she thought he wouldn't accept the change of subject. Finally he spoke. 'I meant merely that you didn't know Imran as intimately as someone who'd grown up with him.'

Asim's mouth curved reminiscently. 'Let me tell you about my cousin. He could climb before he could walk and he never walked when he could run. His nickname in the family was "Trouble" because he was always in strife. Luckily he had nine lives, like a cat, because he was regularly falling off roofs or down wells or under horses. He took risks others wouldn't.'

'Even you?' Jacqui couldn't imagine Asim being left behind by his cousin.

'I never seemed to collect the injuries Imran did.'

So, they'd been as bad as each other.

'When he got older he found a passion in rally driving.'

'I've seen the photos.' Jacqui smiled wistfully. Imran had looked in his element, dusty, dishevelled and elated, leaning against a car that looked as if it had barely survived the rigorous course.

'It wasn't till he went to college and discovered a love of cameras and film that he became focused. He found his purpose. Some of those stories he got…' Asim shook his head. 'He didn't get them waiting on the sidelines to be assured it was safe.'

Reluctantly Jacqui nodded. Imran had been up to any challenge when it came to getting a story. That had drawn them together in the beginning. She'd put it down to his commitment to his job, but had there been an element of thrill-seeking too?

Of course there had been. But Imran had also been professional, taking appropriate precautions in risky situations, at least when she was around.

'At first I wanted to blame you for his death. I was looking for a scapegoat.' Her breath snared as he voiced the guilt she'd carried so long. 'But I couldn't do it. It just didn't fit.' He paused, his eyes capturing hers. 'You can't tell me my cousin would have waited for you to reconnoitre the situation alone.'

Jacqui blinked. When Asim put it like that... But the fact remained it had been her tip-off, her responsibility. 'I led him into danger.' She swallowed.

'No.' Asim shook his head. 'You told him what you'd learned. If he'd wanted, he could have turned back. Couldn't he?' His eyes held hers. 'Jacqueline?'

'I suppose.'

'Is it likely he'd have waited for you to go off alone and track down the story?'

Under that unblinking ebony stare Jacqui found herself confronting the harsh truth.

'No.' The word burst out. 'No, he wouldn't have waited. But that doesn't mean I feel any less guilty.'

'Because you survived and he didn't.' Asim's arm curved around her shoulders, drawing her into his warmth. 'He didn't die because of you, Jacqueline, but because someone cared more for their own ends than the lives of innocents.'

'I—' She shook her head, her mouth working.

'It's okay to grieve for him, *habibti*, so long as you understand you're not to blame.'

Jacqui huddled into Asim's big frame, drawing comfort. What he said wasn't new, the counsellor had said something similar, but for some reason it seemed to make more sense. Because Asim had known Imran? Because they were here in the desert Imran had loved? Or because Jacqui was finally ready to move on?

She buried her face in Asim's sweater, breathing in the spicy scent of his skin. Tears leaked beneath her eyelids and she wrapped her arms around him, holding tight as he gathered her in and rocked her.

Jacqui drew a shuddering breath.

She'd come out here because Asim had broken her heart. Now it felt like he'd put it back together again.

CHAPTER FOURTEEN

'It's utterly gorgeous.'

Asim watched Jacqui's eyes widen as she stepped into one of the rooms at the old royal pavilion. She turned slowly, taking in the delicately coloured wall murals and the shallow pool in the centre of the floor, now dry, that glittered with a mosaic of semi-precious stones.

She walked to the wide seats running the length of the walls, dragging her fingertips over the silk cushions, exclaiming over the fine fabric and delicate embroidery.

She was so tactile, so sensual. Asim remembered the way she stroked his flesh or tangled her fingers in his hair whenever they lay together. How, even when physically spent, he enjoyed those soothing caresses.

Regret pierced him. He wasn't ready to give her up.

If anything, understanding her better and admitting his faults to her as they sat by the fire in the early hours had made her more rather than less appealing. His body craved her with undimmed urgency.

How long before this attraction waned? Weeks? Months? He'd never had a relationship like this. It was new territory.

Asim folded his arms as she pushed open a window and leaned out to take in the oasis view. She wore jeans and a rumpled shirt, her hair loose around her shoulders, and he couldn't take his eyes off her.

No wonder his scheme to find a bride had come to naught! He was bewitched by Jacqueline Fletcher.

It had been a mistake, trying to vet well-bred beauties when he was enthralled by this tawny-haired lioness.

She fascinated him. He'd never known a more contradictory woman—brave when standing up for others or for her work, yet vulnerable and unsure of herself. Responsive and generous, yet abrasive when she thought she was being dismissed.

'It's like an Arabian Sleeping Beauty's palace. There are even roses climbing up the wall. You can smell them.' She turned. 'I wonder if they're the ones the women used to make perfume? Did I tell you about that in Zeinab's diaries?'

'You told me. But I suspect they gathered petals from the palace gardens. There used to be acres set aside for roses.'

'Were there?' She frowned. 'I didn't know. There's so much I haven't had time to finish researching. But I'll make do. If it's okay, I'll call your staff sometimes to check details.'

'Why not check them yourself here?'

Her gaze caught his, a flare of amber that scorched before sliding away. 'It's best if I leave. After last night you don't want…'

'What don't I want?' He paced towards her, watching the tension creep up her shoulders and neck.

'You made it clear we—'

'I made it clear I'd been a fool and that I regret it.' He stopped close enough to note the quick rise of her chest.

Her eyes darted to his, surprise clear in their depths. Asim's mouth quirked mirthlessly. 'Fool' wasn't a word he used of himself but last night it had been true.

And he'd be a fool to let her leave when there was still such pleasure to be gained from their affair. Asim was a man whose life was ruled by duty but he wasn't into unnecessary self-denial. What they had was too good to throw away.

'Stay in Jazeer and finish your work, Jacqueline. Write your book.' He brushed the hair from her face, sliding his fingers over her satiny cheek to cup her face. He felt her tiny tremor and saw her eyelids flicker and knew she wanted this too. 'Stay with me.'

Jacqui looked into that harsh, beloved face and felt torn in two. She wanted to snuggle close and agree to whatever Asim wanted. But last night had revealed with devastating clarity the dangers of their relationship. When he'd turned on her, it had cut her to the core.

She'd never had a lover before. Maybe that was why she felt so…connected? She'd never been so drawn to a man, never trusted one as she'd trusted him.

Surely it was dangerous to give so much? Life had taught her to expect rejection. That she wasn't the sort to inspire love or long-term relationships.

'You're thinking too much.' His fingers rubbed her brow. 'Stop analysing, *habibti*. Can't we agree to make the most of what we have?' He leaned in and kissed the corner of her mouth, teasing her with the promise of more. Inevitably, longing awoke.

Jacqui leaned back, bracing her hands on his upper arms, only to find that gave him access to her throat. Ruthless as he was, Asim didn't hesitate to kiss her there, nuzzling each sensitive spot till her knees wobbled and her nipples peaked.

'Don't! I need to think.'

Dark eyes held her. 'Then think about how good we are together. About the pleasure we give each other.'

His voice was mesmerising. She felt it reverberate deep in her belly, felt her caution splinter.

'Do you want to give that up?'

She shook her head before realising. His smile, pure satisfaction, warned her she'd given away too much.

'But I think some distance would be sensible.'

Asim scowled. He really was used to getting what he wanted.

'What's to be gained by separating? We're good together.'

'There are more important things in life than sex.' Asim

overwhelmed her; he had from the first, with his earthy sexuality and potent charm.

'Don't we share those too?' His eyes narrowed to gleaming slits. 'Don't we swim together and play chess; debate politics, current affairs and literature?' He paused. 'I've never spent half the night just talking with a woman. I've never shared so much of my life.'

Asim's face was grim and Jacqui knew he remembered those revelations about his family.

Suddenly it struck her how out of character that had been. He'd been brought up to be Sultan, raised for the solitary role of ruler, shouldering vast responsibilities and keeping his own counsel. Being dictatorial came naturally. Yet with her he'd stopped to listen, even changed his mind on some things, like giving her access to those diaries. He'd trusted her with information she guessed he'd shared with no one else, like those childhood memories and his fears for Samira.

How could she not be moved by that?

Maybe he cared more than she realised. Was that why he wanted her to stay?

Jacqui tried to squash an urgent buzz of excitement that maybe Asim felt as she did.

She waited but he said no more. Should she walk away, preserve her heart and find sanctuary elsewhere?

Or was it too late?

Had she already gone too far?

Fear spiked, pinioning her where she stood.

'Jacqueline?' His hands tightened on her arms.

It should have made no difference but she couldn't help thinking how much she'd miss the sound of him saying her name in that deep, honeyed-coffee voice if she left.

'I'll think about it.' She bit her lip, knowing she prevaricated.

Asim frowned. Clearly he wanted more.

So did she. Badly.

Finally he released her. Instantly she felt bereft. How could she want his touch even as she feared it was wrong to stay?

'Think about it here. We'll stay a few days and I'll show you the desert.'

Jacqui goggled. 'A few days? You can't do that. What about your meetings? Your schedule?' Any idea she might have harboured about his royal role being a sinecure had been shattered by the sight of his daily schedule. Often he didn't stop work till late evening.

Which meant the time he'd devoted to her really *had been* precious.

Perhaps she was being naïve, expecting more when she already had so much.

'I'd planned some down time after last night's celebration. There will be some appointments to move and arrangements to make if we're to stay here.' Already he was pulling out his phone. 'Leave it to me.'

The sun was setting, its peach and cinnamon blaze gilding the oasis as they rode back from the desert.

Jacqui's blood tingled under her skin from excitement and exertion. Her mare snorted and she laughed in sheer delight.

'I knew you'd make a good horsewoman.'

'Sweet talker!' She turned to Asim, so at ease in the saddle beside her. He looked relaxed, his smile making something flutter high and hard in her chest.

How precious this day had been. She didn't want it to end. 'I suspect your teaching, and the fact you chose such a well-mannered horse, had something to do with it.' She leaned forward, whispering to the mare. 'You wouldn't let me fall, would you?'

'You underestimate yourself. With more practice, you'll be a very good rider.'

Jacqui smiled. 'The only thing that will surprise me is if I can walk when I dismount. I suspect I'm going to be stiff and sore from my first ride.'

'Don't worry. A warm bath and a slow massage will do the

trick. I'll take care of it personally.' Asim's eyes glowed with promise and Jacqui didn't have it in her to argue. Under that look she melted, her very bones liquefying.

All day he'd kept his distance and all day she'd chafed at his restraint.

So much for caution.

They'd spent the day exploring the faded finery of the royal pavilion—a sprawling building designed for short retreats. They'd swum in oasis pools and explored caves in a nearby hill where archaeologists had found evidence of an ancient settlement. They'd picnicked lavishly by the oasis, courtesy of staff who'd driven from the city to make the old place comfortable. Then Asim had given her a riding lesson on the most beautiful Arab mare.

'It's been a magical day, Asim. Thank you!'

'I'm glad you've enjoyed yourself.' The warmth in his expression made the air catch in her throat.

Her resolve to keep her distance had shattered as they'd shared their day. Somehow that proved more intimate than love-making, especially after their campfire revelations. The last twenty-four hours, even Asim's accusations and apology, had drawn them closer.

Jacqui couldn't stop wondering if for Asim, too, this was more than a fling, more than convenient sex.

Had it ever been that for her? She'd tried to tell herself so, but from the first this had been about far more than simple need. It was all about Asim and the wondrous way he made her feel.

They stopped by the stables and Asim swung down, passing his reins to a servant.

'Let me help you.' Moments later she was in his arms, pressed to the steady beat of his heart. His eyes met hers and Jacqui knew it was useless to pretend. She'd crossed the point of no return weeks ago, possibly the night Asim had first made love to her, all the while lavishing her with praise and whispered endearments.

Or perhaps it had been earlier, when she'd seen him with Lady Rania, proud yet patient and protective, revealing an emotional bond that told her he was a man capable of caring deeply.

Or even when they'd argued about her being in the palace—having access to things that had never been shared with an outsider. There was something about sparring with Asim that made her feel vibrantly alive.

She curved her hands around his neck and leant close as he nodded to the stable hand and strode towards the main building. She'd never grow tired of how precious she felt, scooped up in his arms. As if she was some delicate treasure.

It was too late to walk away. The die was cast. She'd give him what he wanted, what they both wanted.

There was only so much a woman could take.

Asim's mobile phone rang as their bath water cooled. His gaze shifted to the bedroom and he frowned.

'Answer it,' she urged, forcing herself to lift her head from his solid shoulder. 'It must be important.'

Lolling in the massive sunken bath, her body lax and deliciously replete, Jacqui couldn't begrudge him his call. In the time she'd known him, this was the longest Asim had gone without a meeting. After the first flurry of calls this morning to arrange his time away from the capital, his private line had been silent as he'd devoted his time exclusively to her.

'Possibly.' But he leaned in to kiss her full on the mouth in a lush caress that liquefied her already weak limbs. Then gently he put her aside to stand, water sluicing down the strong planes of his body.

Jacqui's eyelids dropped to half-mast as she took in the display of masculine perfection before her. Too soon, though, he'd grabbed a towel and, grinning at her reaction, strode from the room.

'I'll wait for you in the bedroom.'

She sighed and wondered if it were possible for this day to

get any better. It had started abysmally but now she felt like she floated on cloud nine.

Finally she made herself move, getting out and wrapping a fluffy bath sheet around her. She was towelling the ends of her hair, walking towards the open bedroom door, when she heard Asim.

'No, cancel the princess's visit.' He paused. 'I know it's short notice but I've had second thoughts. It can't go ahead.' A longer pause. 'No, not her either. I'll explain when I'm back, but for now put the whole schedule on hold. No more eligible women.'

Jacqui paused and looked over her shoulder to where Asim spoke on the phone. He stood, magnificently bare-chested, wearing only a stark white towel around his hips.

His eyes caught hers and something about his expression made her still. She couldn't put her finger on it. Tension? Worry? Determination?

Misgiving feathered cool fingers across her nape. Something wasn't right.

She turned away and reached for a comb, tidying her damp hair while he finished the call. Even then she waited a few extra moments before entering the bedroom, unable to shake a sense of foreboding.

'All finished?'

'Yes.' Asim turned away and took his time putting the phone on the bedside table. She couldn't read his face. For some reason that only added to her nebulous anxiety.

'That sounded intriguing. No more eligible women?' Jacqui put a smile she didn't feel in her voice.

Asim turned, faint colour washing his craggy cheekbones. 'No.'

Warning became a nagging bite of worry. It wasn't like Asim to be monosyllabic. When he said no more, Jacqui turned towards the wardrobe. She wouldn't push.

'I should tell you.' He paused. 'Even though it's ended now.'

Jacqui spun around. 'What's ended?'

Asim palmed the back of his neck as if massaging tight

muscles. The action drew attention to the formidable strength
in his biceps and shoulder, and the musculature of his torso.

They'd been lovers for weeks and still Jacqui was distracted
by the sight of him.

'You might want to sit.' He gestured to the wide bed. Instead
Jacqui sank onto a nearby sofa. Instinct urged against lolling
on a mattress when Asim had news for which she needed to
sit. Unease rippled again.

'I'm thirty-five,' he said, pacing, then turning to face her.
'The last male of my family.'

She nodded. The Sultanate of Jazeer had been in the hands
of the same family for hundreds of years. She'd been fascinated by the way a modern state was melded to such ancient
tradition, like the right of one man to rule.

He walked towards her, stopping less than a metre away, so
she had to tilt her head up.

'I've been looking for a wife.'

Jacqui felt the air rush into her lungs in a gasp. Her eyes
bulged. Finally she forced herself to exhale, ignoring the way
her head spun.

Was it really so surprising?

Yet shock sank claws of steel into her defenceless body.

'You want an heir.' Of course he did. He needed to secure
the succession. Wasn't that what they called it?

Yet for some reason the air seemed suspended in her lungs
and tightness banded her ribs. It might be logical but that didn't
lessen the impact of his bombshell.

'And a spouse. A family.' He paused. 'I've been putting off
the day for years, far too busy enjoying myself when I was
younger, and more recently dealing with the business of government.'

Jacqui sat back, letting the couch support her wilting frame.
Asim and…a wife? She worked to swallow a knot in her throat.

What did this have to do with her?

At the back of her mind a tiny flicker of an idea ignited, but
ruthlessly she blanked it out, refusing to let herself go there.

This wasn't some fairy tale, not with Asim looking so sombre. She knotted her hands in the thick, plush towelling on her lap.

'No questions?' he probed.

Hundreds of them. She settled for the most obvious. 'Why tell me now?'

Again that tiny flare of excitement she couldn't quite extinguish. But, reading his body language, Jacqui sensed there was nothing for her to be excited about. Anxiety drew every tendon and muscle tight.

Asim slowly exhaled and, despite everything, she had to work to keep her eyes on his face.

She was lost and she knew it. Too late now to think of drawing back to protect herself.

'For weeks I've been checking out prospective brides. Almost from the night you arrived.'

Jacqui couldn't stop the abrasive laugh that burst out. 'But obviously not because of my arrival.'

The steely gleam in his eyes confirmed it and that tiny, optimistic spark burnt itself to a lifeless cinder. She knotted her hands, willing her lip not to tremble.

'No, I was in a temper that night because someone had let the cat out of the bag. I'd been faced with some very obvious match-making in a very public situation.'

'And you didn't like the prospective bride.'

His nostrils flared. 'I wouldn't touch her with a barge pole.'

It was stupid to experience an easing of the pain cramping her chest at his words. But Jacqui didn't want him attracted to anyone but her.

Then the import of his words sank in.

'You've been *checking out* women all the time we were…?' She swallowed convulsively, tasting rising bile.

Quickly he took the seat beside her, turning towards her. But he didn't touch her. How telling was that?

Jacqui blinked, her mind reeling. Half an hour ago he hadn't been able to keep his hands off her. And she'd been just as greedy. After believing they'd lost each other last night, their loving had been urgent and phenomenally satisfying. The way he'd held her afterwards, collapsed against his chest in the cooling water, she'd felt the epicentre of his attention. She'd even got a fillip of delight at the idea this retreat to the desert was as romantic as a honeymoon!

'Don't look like that!'

'Like what? Like a woman you played for a fool?'

Asim clasped her hands before she could pull away.

'It wasn't like that.'

From somewhere Jacqui dredged up hauteur, anything to conceal the splintering pain.

'No? What *was* it like, Asim?'

'It was long planned.' He lifted one shoulder. 'I decided what I wanted in a bride and my advisors came up with a list.'

'How very methodical.'

This time both shoulders rose and fell. 'How else could I do it? It wasn't as if I was going to fall madly in love.' His mouth kicked up at one side in a bitter smile that twisted her heart. 'Besides, it wasn't just about choosing a wife but a queen. I'd be stupid not to think carefully and make the right decision.'

Jacqui pressed a hand to her chest, trying to sort her tangled emotions. Hurt pride and savage disappointment were easy. Harder to deal with was the sensation deep in her soul that she'd sustained a critical injury from which she wouldn't recover. There was even part of her that understood Asim's logic.

'So all those royal dinners and receptions…' She stopped, remembering the parade of beauties at his side. She'd spoken to some of them, articulate, sophisticated women who came from a completely different world from hers.

Just as Asim did.

The realisation was a punch to the belly that made her gasp.

'Jacqui?' He raised his hand to her face and she reared back.

'Don't!' She drew a sharp breath, then another. 'So I wasn't supposed to care that you were sleeping with me while you *courted* other women?' It was an old-fashioned word but it implied an intrinsic respect that had obviously been lacking in their affair.

'I never courted any other woman.' His voice grated. 'I never got further than meeting them. I wasn't interested in any of them.'

Jacqui laughed, the sound a broken rasp. 'I'm sure your advisors have plenty more candidates. Let me guess. All from fine, Middle Eastern families, with excellent breeding and the best possible education, all—'

'What would you have had me do?' Asim burst out, his hold on her tightening. 'Look in the soukhs and back alleys for a bride? Of course I searched for someone who'd be personally compatible as well as someone who could handle official royal duties.'

The devil of it was he was right. Wasn't that what royals did, arrange dynastic marriages?

She drew a shuddering breath and looked towards the window framing the view of the oasis. The sky was indigo now. Her day of magic was over.

'I never meant to hurt you, Jacqui. You must know that.' This time when he palmed her cheek she didn't have the strength to pull away. She shut her eyes and told herself soon she'd gather the will to move.

'What's between us…it wasn't planned. You felt it too, that spark that drew us from the first. It kept getting stronger and stronger. I hadn't planned to take a lover, now of all times, but resisting became impossible. You know it.' He tilted her chin.

She opened her eyes and lost herself in the velvet depths of his gaze. Her heart felt bruised and battered and so full she thought it might burst.

'I've never lied to you.'

'Except by omission.'

Gravely he regarded her. 'You're right. It was dishonourable of me. I tried to pull back but I couldn't resist you. You were always *there*, in my consciousness, and no matter how I tried I couldn't keep fighting temptation.' He shook his head.

'I sound like a kid making excuses! The truth was, after that first night, the night I seduced you, I hadn't a hope of putting you aside. You're in my blood.'

His hands moved to her shoulders, as if to prevent her moving.

If he only knew. Nothing on this earth would make her shift now.

For all the hours they'd spent talking, Asim had never spoken so frankly about his feelings. It was as if he shied from admitting softer emotions.

How did he see their relationship? Lust? Friendship with benefits? Or something more?

'And now?' Her voice was stilted by tight vocal cords. 'What happens now, Asim?'

His hands curled around her shoulders in a rhythmic caress. He leaned in.

'I've told my staff to cancel all arrangements to meet...' He stopped, as if choosing his words carefully. 'Anyone else. It was a foolish idea.'

Jacqui's heart soared as she read the warmth in Asim's eyes.

'It's impossible to consider potential brides when you and I have this.' One hand slid across her bare shoulder to stroke the sensitive skin of her neck.

'Really?'

'What do you expect?' His mouth edged up in a smile. 'You're a lover who'd distract any man, Jacqueline. It's nonsense even to think of such things while we're together.'

Jacqui stiffened, her brain chugging into gear despite the distraction of Asim's caresses.

While we're together. Was she imagining it or did that imply an end date?

'So you want to keep me as your lover?'

His brow knotted. 'Of course! What we have is rare. I've never had this with any woman.'

'For how long?' Her lips felt stiff.

'However long the passion lasts.' His smile was taut as he

stroked her neck. He plunged his fingers into her hair, massaging her scalp in a sensual caress that turned her to jelly. 'What we have is too good to give up yet.'

Yet.

Despite the desire to loll back against his touch and let him seduce her into ecstasy, it wasn't going to happen. Not this time.

She hadn't slept with Asim expecting him to declare undying devotion. Like him, she'd been overwhelmed by the force and physicality of their passion. But always there'd been another element for her. Something more profound. Something she'd done her best to ignore.

Something that was all about emotion.

She could ignore it no longer. Not when it sliced her in two, knowing Asim relegated her to the role of sexual partner. Or was the word 'mistress' when the man you slept with ruled a country?

With strength she hadn't known she possessed, Jacqui ripped herself from his hold and surged to her feet, stumbling out of his reach. She pressed a hand to her roiling stomach where her lunch threatened to rise.

'Thank you for explaining where I stand.' Her words were sharp as broken glass. 'It's good to have it spelled out.' It wasn't good; it was a raw, bleeding wound that made her want to curl up in a ball and die.

'Jacqueline?' Asim looked astonished. Was he really so sure she would be content with his scenario? Of course he was. She'd fallen into his arms like a ripe plum.

'So I'm good enough for an affair but not for anything more lasting. Just a bit of sex on the side.' Fury warred with hurt.

He catapulted to his feet. His dumbfounded look would have made her laugh if her throat hadn't seized up.

'It's not like that!'

'Isn't it?' Her hands found her hips through the towel swathed around her. Out of the depths of her anguish came a strength she hadn't known she possessed. It ran like fire through her veins, urging her on to blast him with the truth.

'If it's not like that, then let me suggest an alternative arrangement. Instead of testing all those aristocratic beauties, why not marry *me*?'

Her pulse thudded so loud she could barely hear herself speak but she refused to back down.

'I can offer something they can't. I'm in love with you.'

CHAPTER FIFTEEN

IN LOVE?

Asim formed the words but no sound escaped.

His eyes bulged and something slammed into his chest. Dazed, he looked down but there was nothing, no projectile, no wound. Yet it felt like he'd been shot. He felt the impact spreading through his torso, a shockwave that would have floored him if he'd been standing.

In love.

The words conjured every nightmare memory. They were his worst fear made real.

Jacqueline was speaking. He watched her lips move, heard a harsh rip of sound, but couldn't make out the words.

He stared into her flushed face and read the fierce intensity of her amber gaze. Anguish and defiance glittered in equal measure, flaying him where he sat.

What had he done?

An instant later he was on his feet, stalking to the door, then the window, then back.

She was silent now, looking at him with huge, shadowed eyes.

'You don't mean it.' She couldn't.

But Jacqueline didn't play games. From the first she'd been open, not coy. What you saw was what you got. No feminine wiles.

She stood watching him, her eyes too big in her face, her

damp hair tousled round her shoulders and a bulky towel wrapped around her slim body. Yet she looked more regal than any of the aristocratic women his advisors had selected.

She looked at him as if he was something unsavoury she'd inadvertently stepped in.

'I don't say what I don't mean.' That throaty voice played havoc with him.

Asim shook his head, trying to clear it, telling himself there'd been a mistake.

There'd been a mistake all right!

He'd been so caught up in his need for her, giving in to the fever of attraction, he hadn't been able to keep his hands off her. Even when he'd realised how little sexual experience she had.

Instead of pulling back or taking time to make the ground rules clear, he'd thrown himself into their affair with a single-mindedness he couldn't remember experiencing.

But Jacqueline wasn't like his usual lovers— experienced, sophisticated, ready to move on when the time came, even if some of them had been a little wistful.

Jacqueline was from a different mould.

They said women confused sex and love. Was that what had happened? Perhaps she'd imprinted some fanciful, romantic dream on him because he'd been the one to open her eyes to sensual pleasure.

Asim swiped his hand over his jaw, the rasp of stubble loud in the aching silence.

Why hadn't he taken better precautions? This was the sort of emotional minefield he'd sought to avoid all his life.

Perhaps because he hadn't wanted to know what she felt, in case it meant leaving her before he was ready?

Guilt thwacked him across the chest. But there was indignation too. He'd never once intimated their affair might turn into something permanent. He hadn't encouraged such notions.

But nor had he taken the precautions he should have.

'I'm sorry, Jacqueline.'

The colour bled from her face, making her smattering of

freckles stand out. She didn't look regal now. She looked like a kid who'd been bullied. Or a woman dealt a fatal blow.

Instinctively he started towards her, his gut burning with guilt, but she shoved out a hand, palm towards him.

'No!' She gulped. 'Don't.'

Asim watched her breasts jump with each jagged breath. Each scrape of her breath scored his conscience.

He'd been intent on pleasure and she'd been...

Hell!

He spun away to pace the room.

'I never meant this to happen.'

'So you don't love me.' Her voice was surprisingly strong. He turned to find her backed up against the window, as if trying to get as far as possible from him. His belly cramped on the thought.

But he couldn't lie. 'I already told you. Love isn't for me. I've seen too much of the damage it does.'

'So you couldn't...' she paused then breathed deep '...come to love me?'

How proud she looked. Even now, laying herself on the line like this.

Slowly Asim shook his head. Regret and guilt ran through him like a knife through ripe fruit. He'd never believed it could happen, but he almost wished he *could* love her. He hated what he had to say. And that he had to say it to *her*.

'I care for you more than I've ever cared for any woman, Jacqueline. I admire you. I like you. You're one of the most remarkable people I've ever met.' His voice vibrated with regret. 'But don't look to me for love. You'll never find it. I was inoculated against it at an early age. My parents did that. Growing up watching love tear them apart and almost destroy Samira and me...' He shook his head. 'It's impossible. I'm sorry.'

'And what if you're wrong? What if it wasn't love that destroyed them?'

She stepped forward, eyes blazing. 'Just because your parents were self-absorbed and caught in a destructive relationship doesn't mean love is like that.' Her fisted hands jammed onto her hips, pulling the towelling fabric tight against her slim figure.

Her passion called to him as it always had. He wanted to snatch at it, hold her close and burn in the fire that inevitably flared between them.

Except he knew it for lust, and she believed it to be something altogether more dangerous.

Asim ran his palm around the back of his neck where tendons pulled so tight pain pounded the back of his skull.

'Whatever you call it, I don't want it. I never will.'

Did she sway or was it a trick of the light? Asim braced ready to catch her.

But Jacqueline was made of sterner stuff. She wrapped her arms around her torso in a way that spoke of pain but she stood firm.

'You believe you'll never fall in love?'

It hadn't happened yet. Asim opened his mouth to say so then thought better of the words. He'd hurt her enough. 'It's not possible.'

She bit her lip. To hold back words, or a cry of distress? Asim might be incapable of love but he was no ogre. He cared for this woman, respected her. The sight of her pain was impossible to bear.

'Jacqueline…'

'So you can't offer your wife love.'

He frowned, his outstretched hand dropping to his side.

'No. Not that.' There would be respect and liking, and sex of course, but his bride, when he chose one, wouldn't expect hearts and flowers in a dynastic marriage.

'I see.' She turned and leaned against the window, her neat profile clear against the night sky. Asim's gaze lingered on the smooth curve of her shoulder and the supple turn of her calves beneath the voluminous towel. She was like a creature of moonlight, endlessly enthralling.

He turned away. He had to end this now.

'I have a proposal.'

'Yes?' He swung back.

She laughed briefly and the mirthless sound made the hair on the back of his neck shiver. 'A real proposal.' She turned from the window to face him, her hands straight at her sides like a guard on duty. 'Save yourself the time and bother of interviewing all those women and marry me anyway.'

Asim stared. He couldn't be hearing this.

'I'm not a princess or an aristocrat but there are more important things.' Her slender throat worked as she swallowed. 'I'm intelligent and well-read. I speak your language and I'm getting more fluent every day. I'm loyal and honest and I can be discreet. You know that. I'm even-tempered.' She shrugged and the ghost of a smile skated across her lips. 'Most of the time I'm even-tempered.'

She paused, her eyes searching his, and he wanted to tell her to stop, not do this to herself, to him. But before he found the words she continued.

'I'm a quick learner and with help I'll pick up what I need to know about royal etiquette and protocol. Your grandmother likes me and Samira too. I'm sure they'd help.' This time her smile was real if faint. 'Samira would help me learn to dress the part. And I'm good with people; you know that. I can hold my own at your fancy receptions and with more time I'll learn not to flinch at the sound of fireworks or a twenty-one-gun salute.'

'Jacqueline—'

'I'll make a good wife,' she said in a rush. She clasped her hands tight and he couldn't dispel the uneasy sense that she pleaded with him.

Asim didn't want that. It made him feel wrong inside. His gut, his chest, cramped. His vocal cords froze.

She stepped closer, her tone earnest.

'I'll give you the children you want and you'll always know I'll have your best interests at heart. None of those other women care for you like I do. That must count for something.'

He shook his head, for the first time in his life words failing him.

'Asim—'

'Don't, Jacqueline. Please just...don't.'

Spots of colour appeared on her cheekbones. She stood stock-still, watching him.

'You don't think I'm good enough?' Her voice was ragged and something within Asim nosedived at the pain he heard there.

'It's not that. Never that. How could you think it?' But he remembered her self-doubts and the way trauma had dented her confidence.

He wanted to lie and say it would be okay, that they could marry and she'd be happy. But he respected her too much.

'This isn't about you.' He paced so close he read the tension in her lips and the pain in those over-bright amber eyes. What he saw there almost undid him. He wanted to protect her from hurt. He, who hadn't been able to protect his sister!

'Any man would be proud to have you as his wife.'

'But not you.' Her voice was hollow.

Asim shook his head. 'I'd be proud but I couldn't do it to you. What sort of marriage would it be where you loved and I didn't?' He reached for her then caught himself and pulled his arm back.

'You believe in love, Jacqueline. You *can* love. You deserve the same from the man you marry. You deserve a man who can love you too.' The notion of her with some other man tore a hole through Asim's belly and he almost staggered.

'If we married...' he paused and swallowed, moistening his arid mouth '...it would be unfair and unequal. I'd feel guilty for not giving you what you wanted, not living up to your dreams, and you'd grow out of love eventually. You'd resent me and wish you'd never taken me on.'

'Is that what happened with your parents, Asim?'

'This isn't about them!'

Couldn't she see? Didn't she know she was offering herself

as a sacrifice to a marriage that would destroy her? He couldn't do that to her, despite the selfish part of him that wanted to grab her before she changed her mind.

He breathed deep then regretted it as he caught the scent of apricots. Would that always remind him of her?

'I'm honoured by your offer, Jacqueline. But I can't take advantage of you like that.'

She stepped forward, crowding him. 'I want you to.'

Asim stared into her face, taut with fear and hope, and felt panic that he might weaken. He might not be in love, but he cared for Jacqueline, and he didn't want to leave her.

But he knew his duty to her even if she didn't.

'The woman I marry will not love me, nor I her. It's better that way. Anything else would be unfair on her.' He paused. 'I care for you too much to do that.'

Silence hung between them. Asim couldn't tear his gaze from hers. He wanted to find words to cushion the blow he'd dealt but there were none. He could only protect her by telling her the truth.

Finally she moved, turning her head from side to side like a boxer who'd taken one too many punches.

'In that case, Asim, I'd be grateful if you'd arrange a vehicle.' She looked him in the eye and he felt hurt slam through his chest. 'It's time I left.'

CHAPTER SIXTEEN

THE SUN SHONE BRIGHTLY, turning the park's avenue of old trees into a bower of dappled green light, a welcome respite from Melbourne's summer heat.

But, instead of the neat path and regimented trees, Jacqui pictured the Asada oasis, its crystalline pools and delicious havens of green. When she inhaled she almost smelled the desert sand and spices.

A shout of laughter jerked her head up and she watched a family cross the grass, like so many others heading for the Grand Slam tennis tournament along the Yarra River.

Her eyes lingered on the tall, dark-haired man in the group as he swung a tot onto his shoulders, the other children clamouring for a ride. Then she ripped her gaze away, ignoring the way her chest clamped.

Swerving to avoid them, she set off for the edge of the park. Her hotel was there, across the road, and her hour was up. Each day she forced herself out of the hotel for a walk, to exercise and try to lose herself in the crowds.

Not that it was possible to lose herself. Nothing, not work or the familiarity of her own country, had managed to make her forget, or offer respite from pain. She'd even opted for an anonymous hotel rather than her tiny flat while she finished her book, hoping the novelty might take her mind off the cold weight in her chest.

Jacqui hesitated, wondering if she should try harder. Maybe

order something at the café in the centre of the park and watch the people. Except it was near the Fairies Tree, a mecca for parents with young children.

Jacqui lengthened her stride, heading for the road. When had she become such a grouch that the laughter of children unsettled her?

Since she'd discovered Asim was planning his own family with some other woman.

Jacqui would never bear his child, or hold him close, or have him look at her in that way that made her heart flutter.

She grimaced. That look had merely signified lust. She'd just been too naïve to recognise it.

Had he found his bride? Jacqui had avoided the news, not wanting to hear of a royal betrothal. Pain tore at her throat and roughened her breathing.

With a quick look at the traffic, she stepped onto the road, crossing to her hotel.

That was when she heard the hubbub and saw the security cordon. Jacqui frowned. It was a pleasant hotel with a view over the Treasury Gardens but it wasn't one of the luxury premises visited by VIPs. Yet she saw a news camera beside the entry and a phalanx of staff at the top of the stairs.

Distracted, Jacqui hesitated, then had to scurry to the pavement as a limousine drew to the kerb.

The crowd surged, held back by men in dark suits. The hotel manager hastened from the head of the stairs as the limo door opened.

Curiosity stirring, Jacqui watched a tall figure emerge from the back seat. A figure with wide shoulders and a jacket of steel-grey shot with midnight blue. The slanting morning light caught the rich, matching fabric of his neat turban and accentuated an arrogant slash of a nose that perfectly matched his proud, honed features.

A tingling began in her fingers and toes as numbness swamped her. Even her breath suspended as she took in that oh-so-familiar visage.

Then, in a rush, the blood pounded in her ears and her breath sawed on a gasp that seared her lungs.

She stumbled as she swung around, lurching against a by-stander and almost falling as she willed her feet to keep moving. Anywhere. So long as it was away from here.

Asim, here! What did it mean?

It couldn't be coincidence. For one thing, he'd never mentioned planning a visit to Australia. For another, this wasn't the sort of palatial hotel to house heads of state. For another...

Jacqui couldn't think of another but instinct shouted he was here for her. Why, she didn't know, but she wasn't staying to find out. She wasn't up to treating Asim as a casual acquaintance.

A shout came from behind her. Was that her name?

Jacqui didn't turn but walked faster, clutching her light-weight cardigan around her.

Lights at a crossing flashed green and she hurried across, joining the jostle of pedestrians.

Her heart was hammering, her breath was uneven and her teeth had an alarming tendency to chatter. Swept by the crowd, she scurried along one block then another, until she reached a pavement café. Shock took its toll. Knees rubbery, she dropped into a chair at a table by itself, half-hidden by a planter box.

Jacqui grabbed the menu then laid it down. It shook so badly she couldn't read it. No matter; she'd ask for something sweet and full of chocolate. Something to counteract the shock of seeing Asim.

Had she imagined him? He couldn't really be here.

'Jacqueline.' That deep voice ran like treacle through her body. Instead of stiffening in surprise, Jacqui found herself slumping, exhausted by the inevitable. Had she really thought to escape?

What Asim wanted he always got and for some reason he wanted to see her.

Anger sparked. Couldn't he leave her alone? Couldn't he see she was trying to get on with her life?

Slowly she raised her eyes and flinched as her heart gave an almighty thump of recognition and longing. He towered over her, broad and imposing and impossibly sexy, despite the stark concern etched into his spare features and the grim line of his mouth.

'You shouldn't be here, Asim.'

'I know. I'm supposed to be on a state visit to France.'

'And interviewing brides.' The words jerked out.

Without asking, he took the seat opposite, propping his arms on the table as he leaned close, scrutinising her.

For the first time that day Jacqui gave a thought to her appearance. Hair in a high ponytail, already coming down around her ears, bare of make-up and dressed in lightweight trousers, T-shirt and cardigan, she was hardly prepared for an interview with royalty.

She'd hoped if she saw him again—and she *had* hoped—that she'd look serene, aloof and even beautiful.

Jacqui bit her lip, her eyes lowering.

Asim was the only one who'd called her beautiful.

'Don't.' His hand snaked out and captured hers, clamping it to the table. She gasped as fire sizzled through her veins. The fire she'd told herself she'd imagined. But memory hadn't exaggerated.

One touch from Asim was all it took.

Dimly she was aware of a bustle on the pavement. She turned. Heavy-set security men were trying to block a couple of cameramen from filming. But she noticed a number of mobile phones raised in their direction.

She supposed she should be concerned that he'd made her the subject of gossip just by following her down the street, but that was the least of her concerns.

'You're creating a scene. You should go.'

'I don't give a damn.'

Her eyebrows arched. 'Those are TV cameras. You're making a spectacle of yourself, a target for the sort of stories you hate.'

To her amazement, Asim smiled. The impact rocked her back in her chair and made her forget about trying to wrest her hand free.

'Recent events have put my dislike of the press in perspective.'

'Recent events?' Her stomach plunged and she sat straighter. 'Has something happened to Samira?'

'No, she's thriving, though missing you.' He leaned close and she almost lost herself in the dark velvet of his eyes. 'But there are far worse things than providing fodder for the press.'

Jacqui doubted that. Asim's prejudice was strong. 'Like what?'

'Like losing the one woman in the world who can make me happy.'

His fingers tightened on hers as she recoiled, her spine hitting the back of her seat. The sound of traffic and people blurred to white noise.

'Don't!' It was almost a shout. 'Don't,' she whispered. 'Whatever you're up to, I don't want to be part of it. I walked away, remember? I'm getting on with my life.' No matter that she had yet to discover a spark of interest in anything.

'Oh, I remember, Jacqueline.' His mouth curved in a baring of teeth she could only call ferocious. 'To my everlasting shame, I remember. That's why I'm here. To tell you I'm sorry for what I did, pushing you away.'

Jacqui stared at his harsh expression but hadn't a hope of guessing what he thought.

'It's a long way to come for an apology.'

'You don't think you deserve it?'

She leaned close enough that his spicy scent tickled her nose. Involuntarily she breathed deep, savouring it. Her automatic reaction fuelled an anger she'd hoped had passed. 'What's wrong between us can't be fixed by an apology, Asim.'

To her amazement he paled, the gleam in his eyes extinguished like a flame snuffed out.

'Don't say that.' His hand tightened almost to the point of pain.

'It's true. You want a blue-blooded princess for a cold-hearted marriage. An apology won't change that.' As abruptly as it had flared, her indignation died, replaced by sorrow. 'You can't help what you feel and nor can I. At least you were honest with me at the end.'

His other hand joined the first, engulfing hers on the table.

'That's where you're wrong.'

'Sorry?' Jacqui gaped. Distressed as she was, she knew Asim was a man of his word. Even that last evening, her heart shredding to bleeding tatters, she'd seen his regret. He hadn't wanted to hurt her.

His jaw looked as solid as the stone of the Jazeeri citadel. Only the double-time flick of a pulse at his throat betrayed him.

'Asim?' She was used to him in control, managing every situation, even the business of despatching his unwanted lover.

He didn't look in control now.

'I wasn't honest with you.' The words were a bare rumble of sound, drawing her closer till their heads almost met. 'I told myself I was. I was even proud of myself, in a perverse way, for making us face the brutal truth that we couldn't be together. For bringing everything into the open.'

His nostrils flared on a deep breath and his eyes flickered shut. When they opened again she read something in his expression she'd never seen. It held her trapped as surely as his hands.

Something in her chest seemed to roll over. Her heart?

'I was afraid, Jacqueline. Afraid to face a truth I wasn't ready for.' He swallowed hard. She watched the muscles of his throat work and tried to understand what made him so vulnerable.

One bronzed hand rose to stroke her cheek and it was her turn to swallow as the slow caress evoked sensations she'd thought never to know again. Hot tears glazed her eyes and she fought to stop her mouth crumpling.

'My darling.' His voice was for her ears alone. 'Can you forgive me? I'd spent a lifetime convinced there was no such thing as love, at least for me. I was a coward, terrified to face the emotions you made me feel. I didn't see I'd already fallen for you.'

Jacqui sucked in a stunned breath. 'You love me?' Her heart stuttered then sped to a gallop. She tried to sit back, to digest this, but his hand slid to the back of her neck, warm and compelling, keeping her close.

'I don't deserve you, not after the pain I caused us.' He breathed deep, his chest expanding mightily. 'But I love you, Jacqueline Fletcher. It took me less than a day after you'd left to realise my fatal mistake. I drove you away, not because I didn't care but because I cared too much. I was too cowardly to face that.'

Jacqui blinked. She could read his expression now. It was open and clear. The light she saw there shone like a beacon in the grey that had shrouded her since she'd left him.

'I admire you, *habibti*. I'm fascinated by you, more attracted than I've been to any woman—and I admit there have been a few in my past.' A slashing gesture summarily dismissed them all.

'I care about you. Your happiness is more important than my own. I've never felt that with any woman, but I want only good things for you. I want to spend my life cherishing you and building our lives together. If I hadn't been a coward at Asada I'd have recognised it then.' He shook his head. 'I'd been too busy believing I could control my feelings, never guessing I'd loved you for weeks.'

'You had?' Jacqui was dazed, drinking in his words.

'At least from the night you wore the silver dress.' His eyes glittered with a heat that scorched her from her cheeks to her toes. 'I told myself I was seducing you but all along it was you with your innocence and honesty and courage, seducing me.' He smiled. 'Or maybe it was even earlier. You were in my thoughts all the time.'

Jacqui told herself dreams couldn't come true this easily.

'But I'm not like the women on your list. I'm not aristo-cratic or—'

'You're the woman I want, Jacqueline. No list would do you justice.'

'What about your parents? You said…'

Asim shook his head. 'I said a lot of things. Most of it rubbish. How could I fear what we have together? We're not my parents. You're strong, courageous and loyal and I…' He shrugged those broad shoulders. 'I rely on you to teach me about love.'

Jacqui slipped one hand free and covered his, her heart swelling. 'You're already an expert, Asim. Your love for Samira and your grandmother is there for all to see.'

'Does that mean you'll have me? You forgive me?' His voice, a gravel whisper, dragged like a rough caress across her skin.

'Asim! Are you asking what I think you're asking? Here on a Melbourne street corner?' A bubble of hysterical laughter threatened, fed by shock.

'Why not? Unless you'd prefer I got down on one knee. Is that how it's done here?'

His chair scraped back on the pavement and Jacqui lunged forward, grabbing both his forearms.

'You can't be serious!' She glanced around to see a crowd had gathered, barely held back by his bodyguards. Even the traffic seemed to have slowed and, sure enough, at least one cameraman had his lens trained on them.

'I've never been more serious about anything in my life. I want you as my lover, my wife, my queen.'

'But…' Words failed her. Her heart was so full she felt like laughing and crying at the same time. And hugging Asim and never letting him go. 'But you can't propose here. Look at me: I'm wearing an old *cardigan*!'

Asim's face broke into a smile that stole her breath all over again. 'You'll start a trend, my darling. All the fashionistas will want one in just that shade of brown.'

He stood, pulling her to her feet, his body sheltering her from the crowd.

'Very well, I'll take you somewhere more suitable and ask you to be my bride.' His face sobered, his hold tightening. 'On condition you promise to say yes.'

Jacqui stared up at the one man in the world she'd ever love and understood for the first time that phrase about your heart singing. Hers was doing it right now.

'Jacqueline?' Was that fear in Asim's voice?

She lifted her palm to his face and sighed at the dear familiarity of him.

'That can be arranged, Your Highness. On condition you take me somewhere very, very private. After this…' she gestured to the thronged footpath '…I want you all to myself.'

Asim's eyes glittered with a promise she'd never been able to resist and his mouth curved in a smile of pure satisfaction. Jacqui didn't bother to protest when he scooped her into his arms and strode to the limousine waiting at the kerb.

'I knew this would be a marriage of like minds,' he murmured in her ear. 'Those are my thoughts exactly.'

* * * * *

COMING NEXT MONTH FROM

HARLEQUIN *Presents*®

Available January 20, 2015

#3305 DELUCCA'S MARRIAGE CONTRACT
The Chatsfield
by Abby Green
Happily ever after was never part of this business arrangement, but Giancarlo Delucca finds himself intrigued by his bride Keelin O'Connor's feisty defiance. Now he's determined to turn the beautiful heiress's "I don't" into an "I do"!

#3306 THE REDEMPTION OF DARIUS STERNE
The Twin Tycoons
by Carole Mortimer
Virginal Miranda can't resist the allure of billionaire Darius Sterne. But the closer Darius pulls her, the more he threatens the barriers that conceal the scars of her past. Yet Miranda isn't the only one with pain to hide...

#3307 PLAYING BY THE GREEK'S RULES
by Sarah Morgan
Nik Zervakis lives by his own tenets, and there's no one better to teach Lily Rose how to separate sizzling sex from deep emotions. It starts as a sensual game, but can Lily stick to Nik's rules? And can he?

#3308 THE SULTAN'S HAREM BRIDE
Desert Vows
by Annie West
Journalist Jacqui Fletcher jumps at the chance to write a history of the harem—not to become a sultan's plaything! But it's hard to remember her assignment when Asim of Jazeer's sensuous caresses spark a fire she's never experienced before...

HPCNM0115RA

#3309 TO WEAR HIS RING AGAIN
by Chantelle Shaw

When Isobel sees her husband, Constantin de Severino, again, the temptation to wear his ring once more becomes overwhelming. But as long-dormant secrets are uncovered, Isobel must decide if Constantin is still hers to have and to hold...

#3310 INNOCENT IN HIS DIAMONDS
by Maya Blake

CEO Bastien Heidecker holds Ana Duval's family responsible for the destruction of his own. So he'll satisfy his craving for her, then discard her. But what happens when he discovers that Ana is innocent in *every* sense of the word?

#3311 THE MAN TO BE RECKONED WITH
by Tara Pammi

Even though he's furious that Riya has brought him back to face his past, Nathanial Ramirez can't refuse her bait. Now he'll use every sensual weapon in his considerable arsenal to secure his heritage...and get Riya in his bed!

#3312 CLAIMED BY THE SHEIKH
by Rachael Thomas

Prince Kazim banished his wife from his kingdom long ago but now he needs her back. Amber's always threatened Kazim's tightly held control, yet to save his nation—and his marriage—he must finally make the ultimate claim...on his wife!

REQUEST YOUR FREE BOOKS!

2 FREE NOVELS PLUS
2 FREE GIFTS!

YES! Please send me 2 FREE Harlequin Presents® novels and my 2 FREE gifts (gifts are worth about $10). After receiving them, if I don't wish to receive any more books, I can return the shipping statement marked "cancel." If I don't cancel, I will receive 6 brand-new novels every month and be billed just $4.30 per book in the U.S. or $4.99 per book in Canada. That's a saving of at least 14% off the cover price! It's quite a bargain! Shipping and handling is just 50¢ per book in the U.S. and 75¢ per book in Canada.* I understand that accepting the 2 free books and gifts places me under no obligation to buy anything. I can always return a shipment and cancel at any time. Even if I never buy another book, the two free books and gifts are mine to keep forever.

106/306 HDN FVRK

Name	(PLEASE PRINT)	
Address		Apt. #
City	State/Prov.	Zip/Postal Code

Signature (if under 18, a parent or guardian must sign)

Mail to the Harlequin® Reader Service:
IN U.S.A.: P.O. Box 1867, Buffalo, NY 14240-1867
IN CANADA: P.O. Box 609, Fort Erie, Ontario L2A 5X3

Are you a current subscriber to Harlequin Presents books and want to receive the larger-print edition?
Call 1-800-873-8635 or visit www.ReaderService.com.

* Terms and prices subject to change without notice. Prices do not include applicable taxes. Sales tax applicable in N.Y. Canadian residents will be charged applicable taxes. Offer not valid in Quebec. This offer is limited to one order per household. Not valid for current subscribers to Harlequin Presents books. All orders subject to credit approval. Credit or debit balances in a customer's account(s) may be offset by any other outstanding balance owed by or to the customer. Please allow 4 to 6 weeks for delivery. Offer available while quantities last.

Your Privacy—The Harlequin® Reader Service is committed to protecting your privacy. Our Privacy Policy is available online at www.ReaderService.com or upon request from the Harlequin Reader Service.

We make a portion of our mailing list available to reputable third parties that offer products we believe may interest you. If you prefer that we not exchange your name with third parties, or if you wish to clarify or modify your communication preferences, please visit us at www.ReaderService.com/consumerchoice or write to us at Harlequin Reader Service Preference Service, P.O. Box 9062, Buffalo, NY 14269. Include your complete name and address.

SPECIAL EXCERPT FROM

HARLEQUIN®

Presents®

Harlequin Presents welcomes you to the world of
The Chatsfield
Synonymous with style, spectacle...
and scandal!

Read on for an exclusive extract from
Carol Marinelli's thrilling installment in this
exciting series:

PRINCESS'S SECRET BABY

* * *

PRINCESS Leila of Surhaddi no longer existed.

The elevator took her down to the reception area and
Leila looked around for a moment.

Elegance was the policy at the Harrington and famous
people welcomed that they could be there without fuss.
Such was her beauty, though, such was her way, that people
could not help but look.

She heard the sound of a piano and followed it. As
Leila walked into a bar the chink of glasses and the sound of
subdued conversation dimmed for a moment. She stood in
the doorway in absolute terror, not that she showed it. What
the hell had she even been thinking?

But then *it* happened.

Then, for the first time in her entire life, Leila felt welcome when she walked into a room. A man at the bar turned around and his chocolate-brown eyes met hers. For a brief second he startled and then frowned, as if trying to place her, and then he simply smiled.

Leila had never, not once, felt so welcome. His eyes did not roam her body as other men's had; they simply met and held hers. Leila found that she was smiling back. Then, as naturally as breathing, she walked over to him.

"I've changed my mind," the man said. His voice was rich and expensive and he turned and spoke to the barman. "I'll have another drink after all." Then his eyes returned to Leila's. "What can I get you?"

Her whole life she had been afraid, yet she wasn't now.

* * *

*Step into the gilded world of **The Chatsfield**!*
Where secrets and scandal lurk behind every door…

Reserve your room!
March 2015